"Madeline ffitch is a natural-[ ]oice doesn't just entertain, it illumi[ ]in a cave. No one writes like ffitch.[ ]guts and heart. So real and tactile are these stories that I could smell the weird smells. I saw deep into the blood bonds of family. Trust these brave narrators! Befriend thieves, crawl woods, pick fights, steal cars, study turtles, shoot guns, stay true. Personality is power in this unflinching book; nature does what it will while ffitch's words hum with wisdom."

—RACHEL B. GLASER, AUTHOR OF *PEE ON WATER*

"I've spent years enjoying Madeline ffitch's words, encountering stories here and there, watching performances of her plays, but even all that delight couldn't prepare me for the total joy of reading her first full-length book. These superb stories are an excellent introduction to ffitch's distinctive sensibility: lively, curious, socially-engaged. She presents us with characters whose kindness, foibles, cruelty, and courage combine to form an expansive image of our imperfect species. Frighteningly observant and deeply funny, *Valparaiso, Round the Horn* feels at once classic and contemporary, like discovering a traditional song that perfectly recounts our current plight. And like that song, ffitch's debut will rouse you, make you feel you are part of something larger, that—whatever our fate—we are headed to meet it together."

—HEATHER CHRISTLE, AUTHOR OF *WHAT IS AMAZING*

"These stories read like tall tales dictated from the future, their narrators enthusiastically discarding the usual interpretations of events, the usual histories of people and place. Skewed, slanted, refracted and remade, Madeline ffitch's America is one of legend, a country of misunderstanding and mistake and sudden majesty that I'm thrilled to have visited."

—MATT BELL, AUTHOR OF *IN THE HOUSE UPON THE DIRT BETWEEN THE LAKE AND THE WOODS*

VALPARAISO,
ROUND THE HORN

Madeline ffitch

PUBLISHING GENIUS
BALTIMORE, ATLANTA

Published by Publishing Genius Press
Atlanta, Georgia
www.publishinggenius.com
First edition February 2015

Copyright © 2015 by Madeline ffitch
All rights reserved

ISBN 13: 978-0-9906020-0-2

Cover art and design by Jessica Seamans, landland.net
Page design by Adam Robinson

Distributed to the trade by Small Press Distribution
www.spdbooks.com

STORIES

For Kurt Joseph Vance, 1951 - 2013, who honored the mysterious, taught me thing-making, encouraged me to tell the true parts of the story

And for Nector Vine

VALPARAISO, ROUND THE HORN

For every construction worker who is a man who pees next to the work area of a construction worker who is a woman and when the woman says "please don't do that. Instead, why don't you pee in the porta-pottie?" and the man says "if you don't like it don't work on a fucking construction site," and the woman complains to her supervisor, who is also a woman, who says "it sounds like maybe you weren't cut out for this kind of work," there is also a construction worker who is a man who is kind of private about where he pees, and would really prefer to pee in the porta-pottie, and who definitely doesn't want to pee on or near a female coworker, although not out of sensitivity so much as out of being sort of conservative about peeing, and such a man was Abie Carlebach.

That spring, Abie worked for Black Rose Construction, between the Lake Union dry dock and the YMCA. Abie enjoyed working near the YMCA because he liked to go swimming, and he enjoyed working near the Lake Union dry dock because of all the sea chanties being sung at odd hours. It was sincere and it was contemporary. The sailors patched the cavernous engine. Abie built condos next door.

Abie was a construction worker who hoped to be left alone, who hoped to just fit in, who hoped to hide up there in the scaffolding, shirking his vision. Someday he hoped to hop on a steel plank being lowered to the ground by crane. Also, to mimic the photo of the construction workers lunching on a crossbeam while building the Rockefeller Center. And Abie knew that he would be too afraid to do either of those things.

Abie worked for two brothers, Murray and Phil, former Black Panthers who were still pretty jumpy because they knew the war against them was not over. Sure enough, on April 13th, a day that was still raining, they were arrested on suspicion of being terrorists or knowing some other people who were terrorists and not telling the authorities about it. Abie knew this was a frame-up. He knew that Murray and Phil had their reasons for living as they did. But his feeling was, what could he do?

Before April 13th, Phil, the younger brother, told him that women might like him better if he said something like this to them: "There's a tiny little owl, the strangest, cutest owl. Yes, it has been appointed the cutest owl, and the strangest owl." If he spoke from the heart. If he asked her questions about herself, questions such as, "Is it cuter, do you think, than those two kittens there, fitted together sleeping like beans?"

"What if there aren't any actual kittens around?" asked Abie.

"Oh, just use your imagination," said Phil.

"What if she asks what the tiny owl is called?" Abie asked.

"Tell her it's called the *xenoglaux*," Phil said. "The Strange Owl."

Before April 13th, Murray, the older brother, told Abie he'd sounded black over the phone, but now they had him they didn't want to let him go because, when he drove the company truck on errands to the lumber yard, he was such a fast and such a safe driver, both at once.

———

At the lumberyard, before April 13th, a white contractor leered at him. "How is it working for that nigger company?" he whispered. Abie was startled. Up until then, he had thought that most white people didn't use that particular word anymore, that it had gone out fashion as the most favored expression of racism. Yet Abie was afraid to hop on a steel plank, he was afraid to lunch on a crossbeam. His mouth dry, he whispered back to the contractor, "Fine. Actually, it's great."

For this, and for other reasons, Abie was embarrassed pretty much all the time. Yet no one seemed to notice. When he went to pick up his pay at the Black Rose construction office, many women who had just had their hair done flirted with Abie good naturedly. Why couldn't he just relax?

Instead, he began to drive faster, and even more safely.

Sometimes, early in the morning, alone in his room, Abie would wrestle with the big questions. He would think, "Why do I work such a physically rigorous job when I have not found my passion? What do I, Abie Carlebach, need money for?" And he would answer himself, "I need money to pay rent on this room, and to eat this delicious sort of food that I like to buy at the grocery store." He liked to eat spaghetti and meatballs, and he liked to roast eggplants over the gas range until they were black. For lunch, he ate egg sandwiches, like most people. "There must be a way around these things, but right now, I haven't found what that way is," thought Abie.

On April 14th, Murray and Phil's mother, Mrs. Rose, took over. Abie felt that she bullied him a little bit. He worried that this was because he was the newest employee, and white, and slight of build. For example, Mrs. Rose came out to the construction site on the morning of April 14th to make sure Abie began work on time. She stood under his scaffolding while he used the nail gun. She looked up at him, and her face was perfectly clean.

"Young man," Mrs. Rose said. "I am under a lot of emotional stress because of what the pigs have done to Murray and Phil. I wish my boys had kept their noses clean. I wish that Murray had kept Phil out of trouble. What can I do?"

"It's a frame-up, that's obvious," said Abie.

She was quite slim, and quite old. "Thank you for your sympathy, young man," she said.

"Do you think there's still a chance for them to escape?" asked Abie.

"Escape to where, young man?"

"You can call me Abie," said Abie.

"Escape to where?"

"Don't you people go to Cuba sometimes?" asked Abie.

"Us people?"

"Ma'am, I think you people are heroes," said Abie.

"It's too late for anyone to go Cuba now," said Mrs. Rose.

"What's your first name?" asked Abie.

"Erica," said Mrs. Rose. She was crying, and she walked away, and she was wearing hiking boots that she had bought specifically in order to do her new job better.

Of course, it was time for a break, and so Abie took out his egg sandwich, and sat on a cinder block. Three of Abie's coworkers were men, and one of them was a woman, and they were black, and they left him alone. He could hear the strains of a sea chanty floating over the fence from the dry dock: *Oh wake her, oh shake her, oh shake that gal with the blue dress on.* He heard the groan of a great chain uncoiling, and just beyond Lake Union, and through the locks, there was always, and also that day, the creak of the sea.

Abie ate his egg sandwich slowly, and soon the Captain came up along the avenue from the dry dock gates. The Captain was a real old salt, a real old tar, an old mariner.

He was the captain of the largest ship in dry dock that spring, The Cutty Sark the Second. He stopped in front of Abie. He wore an ancient oilskin, and a knit cap, and he squinted his eyes around, breathing through his mouth until Abie looked up.

"We'll shanghai you, my boy," said the Captain. "Ha."

Abie had learned not to react, except with curiosity.

"When will you go to sea?" asked Abie.

"We won't go to sea on a Friday, for that's bad luck for sure, but we should have been at sea three months ago. The work goes slowly. I'm not a happy man, Abie. I don't like this fresh water. I taught my crew every song they know, but still, the work goes slowly."

"I like the one about the girl with the blue dress."

"The beautiful whore," said the Captain, "I was in love with her."

"I like that one," said Abie.

"The work goes slowly because all hands have unionized," said the Captain. "I support it and don't support it."

"The Rose family is benevolent. I've never felt I needed a union," said Abie.

"Betraying your class, is it?" said the Captain.

———

The union office was on the fourth floor of the YMCA building. The girl behind the desk wore a nametag that read "Cappy." She had horse teeth, she had a pumpkin jaw, her eyes went twinkle twinkle with what did not turn out to be mischief.

She started right in on him, making him feel like a prude, which he was.

"Do you work with any women?" she asked.

"One of them," Abie said, afraid right away of making a mistake. "She's a black woman."

"So what?"

"I've never spoken to her."

"You've got to talk to people if you want to organize your workplace. You can't just not talk to them. Especially if you're shy. We have a workshop you can take called Organizing Non Shy People for Shy People. It's taught by a person who used to be shy."

"I'm not shy," said Abie, "I talk to my boss a little bit. She's a woman."

"Where do you pee when you're at work?"

Abie felt hot. He felt that he had to pee right then. He wanted to excuse himself. "I pee in the porta-pottie," said Abie. He held it.

"Have you ever peed on the woman that you work with?"

"No. I don't know her very well."

"It happens to women on the work site all the time. They get peed on or near. Haven't you read about it?"

"It sounds terrible."

"It sounds terrible, and it sounds like a lot of other things."

"Like what other things?" asked Abie. He wanted to protect her. Her hair was fuzzy as a baby.

"How about this. Why is it that you've got a room full of men with only one woman, and, on a dime, they all start gang raping this woman? They do this all together, these men."

"Which men?"

"The men who would not do this if they were alone," said Cappy.

"I have read about that, I think," said Abie. "Has that ever—" and then he thought better of it.

"No, it's never happened to me personally. But I work with women who are victims of this," Cappy said. Abie was flooded with relief.

"Have you ever been peed on?" asked Abie.

"No, not personally," said Cappy. "The worst thing is the woman supervisor who is unsympathetic. That's what I think is the worst thing."

"Worse than being peed on?" asked Abie.

"At least pee is sterile," said Cappy.

"Have you heard about the tiny, strange owl?" asked Abie. He wanted to stop right then and talk about why the world is actually made up of moment by moment by moment.

They began to spend time together, so that Abie could talk to her about this, and they went to the aquarium, and to the small park, and to the bigger park, and they went back to Abie's room, and her nipples stuck straight out and were no color at all. When they spent time together with the lights off and some other things, she'd shriek in a voice like china. It moved him. It moved him once, but not the second time. The second time Abie suspected in a rush that she was faking it, and his feelings were hurt. Then he felt guilty for having his feelings hurt. Mostly, he felt the feeling of a cat with his whiskers cut right off. He bumped into the wall. She sat up in bed.

"Have you heard about dolphins?" she asked. "Have you heard about how all dolphin sex is gang rape?"

"I have heard about that," Abie said, "but I don't quite know what it means."

"You identify more with the bosses, don't you, Abie?" asked Cappy.

This took Abie right into May, and it continued to rain, and The Cutty Sark the Second did not put to sea.

Erica Rose visited the construction site once every two days, wearing her hiking boots and wearing a deep green jacket made out of canvas. Abie could see that it wasn't waterproof enough. She took in large shuddering breaths as she walked around the site, checking on things. It was May 21st when she approached Abie again as he ate his egg sandwich again.

"Young man, I hear you've been talking union," she said.

"No, I haven't," Abie said.

"You have or you haven't?" she asked.

"I haven't because I'm too shy," Abie said, "But I would like to, because I think it's the right thing to do. Listen to the sailors next door."

They listened. At that moment, the sailors were singing, *We're bound for Valparaiso round the Horn.*

"That's their tradition," Erica Rose said, "But right now, if you organized, I would go out of business. Is it that big jawed white woman?"

"Yes."

"I don't like her. She's always speaking up for other people."

"She can be difficult," Abie said. "But still, I don't see her as often as I'd like to."

"There are a lot of other women who don't go around making so much trouble for other people. This, while thinking they understand every single thing," said Mrs. Rose.

"How are Murray and Phil doing?" asked Abie.

Their mother said, "Abie, if you are an imprisoned person, there's a secret thing you can do, and I think it's very smart: You wake up a little before it's really time to get up and face another day of imprisonment. Maybe, if you're under heavy surveillance, you keep your eyes closed. Or maybe, if it's a different kind of imprisonment, like just plain old slavery, you open your eyes and look up at the ceiling. But the main thing is, you lie there, in bed, awake, but not getting up yet, and you steal some time for yourself. No one can make you not do this. Any person can make this time for themselves. And what do you think about? Anything you want. That's the point. If you have a brother, you might think about him. You might think about what it was like to grow up with him right beside you all the time. If that's too painful, you might steal time to avoid thinking about your brother, and about how he is a bit younger than you, and how he does everything in a way that is completely correct. He rattles off little bits of useless trivia about animals and local history. He lets his nose run without noticing it for a full minute. This, while giving people romance advice. My boys wake up, and they stay in bed before anyone knows they are awake, and they think about whatever they want to think about, and no one can stop them from doing that."

They looked up and the Captain was there. He took off his cap and looked abashed. He had never met Erica Rose before. Abie introduced the two of them.

"I couldn't help but overhear your sentiments," said the Captain. "I want to tell you the strange fact that when my father was a toddler in Rhodesia, he played with black African slaves, and though technically they were servants, I feel it's more accurate to call them the first thing. It's never sat right with me."

"What do you want me to do about it?" asked Mrs. Rose. They all looked at Abie's sandwich.

"Are you really sailing for Valparaiso?" Abie asked the Captain.

"Yes, my boy. You've got free passage if you want it, though you'll have to sign on as a deckhand and work your way up. We're bound for Chile, where the native whores are fiery and innocent. A combination that slays me."

"I'll take my chances here, thanks," said Abie.

"Don't make up your mind quite yet, my boy. We sail tomorrow, and I'd like the two of you to come aboard tomorrow morning before we weigh anchor, just to have a look around."

"Thanks very much," Erica Rose said. "I'll be there."

"I might be there," Abie said.

The next morning, before work, Abie went swimming at the YMCA. His strongest stroke was the breast stroke, and on his second lap, the swimmer in the lane next to him swerved a bit, so that Abie accidentally kicked her in the stomach. He felt the impact, deep and doughy and slow. Immediately, he began to tread water. But the other swimmer, in a black suit that turned silver when she twisted her body, did the crawl fast and desperate away from Abie. She wore a swimming cap, like any normal person would, what was wrong with that, and she stood up when she reached the shallow end. It was Cappy. Abie hadn't seen her since the dolphin rape day.

"Oh, it's you," said Abie. "I'm sorry I kicked you in the stomach. But you've got to stay in your lane."

Cappy didn't answer. She pointed at Abie, and she waved at the lifeguard. "Lifeguard, I want this man escorted out of this pool. I cannot swim if he is here," she called. It was so brave of her. Abie felt such shame that he couldn't move. Two lanes away, another swimmer stood up. It was the Captain, wearing modest trunks that went down past his bare blue knees. The old salt said, "Don't swim in this fresh water, my lad. Follow me to sea. It's your last chance." They left the YMCA together. "You'll have to eat limes, so as not to get scurvy," said the Captain.

"Naturally," said Abie. He wasn't sure he had the gumption. "What if I get sea sick?" he asked.

"Ah, the *mal de mer*!" the Captain laughed at Abie, and they walked past the dry dock, away from the dry dock, always at sea level, along the shoreline, past stacks of dishes on rooftops, towards the Puget Sound, towards the salt water. The unions had put the dishes on the rooftops as a means of playing a fantastic trick on the bosses, and no food could be served in the restaurants because they had no dishes to serve the food on.

"What do the union men eat out of?" asked Abie.

"The union men eat out of one big pot, and they feel fine. They feel solidarity, which I've heard is the absolute best feeling," said the Captain.

Elsewhere, the unions had hidden all the farm equipment under bales of hay, as another trick on the bosses. All of these tactics worked so well. All of these tactics got the goods.

Abie wanted to join with the other men in yellow raincoats. He knew these men peed on or near women sometimes, but he still wanted to be close to them and hear their glorious plans for the future. When they reached the saltwater, The Cutty Sark the Second was waiting for them. Erica Rose was already aboard.

"I'm not going the whole way," she said, "I just want to have a look around. Maybe have a glass of port in the Captain's cabin."

"I might go the whole way," said Abie.

"That's my boy. We'll pierce a gold ring through your ear when we round the Horn, just in case you should ever drown. Ah, the sea. The great equalizer," said the Captain. "Isn't that right, Mrs. Rose?"

"I'm not a good one to ask about that sort of thing," said Erica. "I have no scruples. In my eyes, everyone I want to be near is equal. They're equal because I want to be near them so much."

"It's just spring fever setting in," said the Captain.

"But it feels so real," Erica Rose said.

They had been at sea for one hour, they were going full speed, they were going eleven knots, when the proud union men cried out, "Porpoises off the starboard side!"

All hands gathered at the bow, and the dolphins leapt all the way over them, all the way up, ten feet up, twisting their bodies in the light and salt spray. Down in the foam, they cut fast through the white water like electricity moves fast. They didn't have any arms, which Abie knew before he saw them, but other species can be so persuasive, you can feel so kindred with them, like they're just humans wearing special suits, and when you think about it that way it becomes a simple miracle that they roll around like that with only their sharp slick fins to propel them.

And that is why I met Abie Carlebach in Chile, and why I fell in love with him, and why I will never at any time feel different.

WHAT WANTS
TO BE SHOT

Even now, no one knows what it was like for Thomas J. Jefferson and Flip J. Jones to be best friends. No one knows what it was like for them that summer, though each day, Hayworth watched their long involved preference for each other. They tried to attract the attention of the songbirds in the ash trees, and they used outdated slurs such as "bulldagger." They used outdated slurs when they stubbed their toes, or when they couldn't get the attention of the songbirds in the ash trees. They hadn't killed anything. They wore matching red trunks, and nothing else. They had turned brown all over their bodies (this was from never going inside) and their legs were impossibly long. Hayworth was Thomas J. Jefferson's girl-cousin, five years younger, and she loved those two young men as if she herself wasn't even real.

They all three of them believed in feats of strength, and so they left the city, and for two days they walked through the long low spindly woods. First, they came through rows of thin white tree trunks, and then they came through leaves like light coins, and finally they came to a four way intersection, arid and still. Here, there were four empty storefronts facing each other, and nothing going on, not even a cat going on, only some raccoons back in the alley, raccoons with dexterous black gloves, like they all have. Each storefront had a stoop, and each stoop was baked hot in the afternoon sun the day they came to the intersection. They all noticed how quiet it was, as quiet as if they'd drawn the place with a crayon as they came along. So they decided to stay there all summer, and the summer was hot. Thomas J. Jefferson and Flip J. Jones had a pair of .22 rifles between them.

"What are we going to shoot with those rifles?" asked Hayworth. She had looped embroidery floss through the holes in her ears, three strands, orange, mandarin orange, and blood orange. Hayworth had occasionally asked for privacy, but when she got it, it was only a coincidence.

"We'll shoot bottles, and we'll throw my old boots up across the telephone wire, and we'll shoot at them, and we'll shoot anything that bothers us," said Thomas J.

"We don't want a thing to bother us," said Flip J. "You can share my ammunition box, Hayworth."

"You'd better not shoot any of that raccoon family," said Hayworth.

"We'll shoot anything that bothers us," repeated Flip J. He was kind, and he showed his large teeth like blocks of ice, and Hayworth loved him.

Hayworth stepped up onto the stoop behind her so that she was eye level with Flip J. Behind her, the Green River Soda marquee was empty, and the screen door hung open, and they didn't know what could be inside.

"It'll stay much quieter here if you don't go galloping around shooting those raccoons for no reason," said Hayworth.

"See, this is what I mean, goddammit, Hayworth," said Thomas J. "We let you come through the woods with us, we let you drink rum and water with us, and by the way, you've given me no reason to regret that. I like having you here, and Flip J. likes having you here."

"I like you a lot, Hayworth," said Flip J.

"But goddammit," said Thomas J, "if you don't sometimes act just like a seventeen-year-old girl."

"Thomas J, all I'm saying is that we could stay here the whole summer, and there would never be any need to shoot a raccoon," said Hayworth.

"Is that a rule you're making?" asked Thomas J. He cut his eyes down away from her. He practiced proper gun safety.

"I'm not afraid to make it a rule, if you want it like that," said Hayworth.

"What's the rule?" asked Flip J.

No one knows what it's like for two boys to be best friends, but we know a few things, gleaned over the years.

We know, for example, that when Flip J. Jones and Thomas J. Jefferson were teenagers, they rode out together one night on a pair of junked bikes, through the city that they came from. Thomas J. pulled ahead, and Flip J. fell behind, though he pushed hard to keep up. We know that Flip J's wheel skidded out. He went over the handlebars, and crunched his head right against the asphalt. It slid, it shaved like a bar of soap. Thomas J. circled back, and when he lifted Flip J. it was bad, it was a stranger he found. Thomas J. taught Flip J. to walk again, and Flip J. learned it good-naturedly and well. Flip J. was rangey and true, and if he didn't like you, you knew it was no use thinking you were any good. Hayworth wanted Flip J. to touch her, and he had never touched her. Yet her cousin, Thomas J. had never protected her from anything.

"The rule is that you can shoot what wants to be shot," said Hayworth.

—

Thomas J. knelt, took aim at the storefront window across the street, and crack, and the window was a spider's web. Flip J. said, "'Atta kid," and meant no harm.

"What about that?" Thomas J. asked.

"That window wanted to be shot," said Hayworth.

"'Atta kid," Flip J. said again. Hayworth took her turn next. What wanted to be shot was a dented folding chair set up at the end of the block. She handed the rifle to Flip J. What wanted to be shot was the upstairs window of the empty five and dime. What wanted to be shot were the red roof tiles above the Green River Soda marquee, the rubble of the ex-sidewalk, the beer cans stabbed onto the chain link fence, the lid of each trash can, an unplugged ice machine, and the knothole of the ash tree that stood on the southwest corner all alone.

By late afternoon, they had gone through Flip J's box of ammunition, and they sat down together to take a rest, Flip J. and Thomas J. on the top step, Hayworth hanging around on the railing. Thomas J. and Flip J. only approved of the liquor that, like burnt sugar, lashed you and was good to take with water. They had some of it now, and they shared it with Hayworth.

"Hayworth would like to marry you someday, Flip J," said Thomas J. Flip J. grinned in his sheepish way. He took a grey dove's feather from the bottom step and twirled it between his fingers. "But I'm too old for her," he said.

"She doesn't care about that," said Thomas J. "You'd better look out."

"Is that true, Hayworth, what your cousin's always saying?" asked Flip J, keeping his eyes on the feather.

"Maybe it is. There wouldn't be any shame in it," said Hayworth. One of the raccoon family, now that the noise and smoke was over, trotted out into the dim intersection. The three of them watched it. Its back was a steep round hump, small and industrious, the moon stood in the sky, and Thomas J. and Flip J. rose at the same time, and crack, crack, and the raccoon flipped over with no noise, and was still. Dark liquid splashed briefly from it, turning the dust to mud.

"I told you not to do it, I told you not to!" said Hayworth.

"You told me what, you stupid kid thought you could make up rules at me out here?" asked Thomas J.

"I asked you not to, that's all," said Hayworth.

"You're lucky you're even here," said Thomas J.

"What about you, Flip J? You know that raccoon didn't want to get shot," Hayworth turned to him.

"It's no big deal, Hayworth," said Flip J, smiling and looking at the ground.

"Now what are you going to do?" asked Hayworth.

"What do you mean?" asked Thomas J.

"What are you going to do with it?" asked Hayworth.

"We'll leave it there as a warning to other raccoons," said Thomas J.

"Raccoons are our blood enemies," said Flip J, affably scratching the back of his head.

"You're just going to leave it there?" asked Hayworth.

"We'll leave it there for a little while, and we'll see if a bigger animal, a scavenger, comes along and eats it," said Thomas J.

"Sure. It's no big deal," said Flip J. He turned his kind face towards Hayworth.

"I asked you not to, that's all," said Hayworth. The rum turned in her stomach.

"I'm tired of this. Let's have a race," said Thomas J, to clear the air. "What should we race to, Hayworth?"

"Shut up, Thomas," said Hayworth.

"Come on, Hayworth, let's race," said Flip J. His sausage lips peeled back uncertainly. He scratched the back of his head again. He looked between the two of them.

"You choose the course, Hayworth," said Thomas J.

"I told you I want you to shut up, please," said Hayworth. They waited for her. She said, "We'll race a mile back through the woods until we get to the white boulder. Then we'll race back."

"Shortcuts?" asked Thomas J.

"Alright," said Hayworth.

"First one back to the dead raccoon wins," said Thomas J. He went off running, his red trunks flashing between the pale ash trees. Hayworth and Flip J. took after him, keeping to the path. Hayworth thought of Geronimo, but Flip J. wanted to talk.

"Hayworth," he loped alongside her, taking one stride for every two of hers, "do you believe that people could run as fast as horses?"

"Yes, I believe that," said Hayworth, loving him. "Why did you kill that raccoon?"

"It was sneaking around too much, and anyway what makes you think it was my bullet, and not Thomas J's?"

"You shot that raccoon, Flip J," said Hayworth, "and now you're just going to let it lie there."

"Raccoons die all the time," said Flip J, "but I don't want you to feel bad. Do you think Thomas J. protects you enough?"

"No. He believes I can stand up for myself."

"He lets you drink rum and water with us on the stoop," Flip J. observed.

"What is it like for you and Thomas J. to be best friends?" asked Hayworth.

"I love Thomas J." said Flip J, "Beyond that, it's like you might think." They ran on awhile.

"Do you think you're too old for me, Flip J?" asked Hayworth.

"Too old for what, Hayworth?"

"Don't be stupid, Flip J."

But Flip J. was not stupid. He had no guile. They ran on in silence, because they believed in feats of strength, and they wanted to beat Thomas J, and they wanted to beat each other. When they arrived at the white rock, Thomas J. had already marked it with a bit of charcoal, and was gone back through the trees. He must have taken the short cut because they hadn't met him on the path. Hayworth swung herself up onto the rock, with silver threaded through it. She pulled at the embroidery floss in her ears. "Well?" she asked. She leaned down towards Flip J. His teeth were sticky and gleaming through the dark.

No one knows what it's like for two boys to be best friends. We will always wonder what they talk about on long journeys when it's just the two of them, but we will never know because no one knows. It's a secret. We have to go by pieces. We know, for example, that it's nice to have a pal in your corner, and sometimes you don't even have to talk about it. Sometimes, if you get in a fight, you can just go off into the woods together and box it out. You don't have to talk about it, you just box it out, back in the thin ash woods, back by the raccoon hide-out, where the raccoons wash their stolen food in pools of water, those bandits, those aristocrats.

Flip J. put his head up, and Hayworth leaned down, and they kissed like two animals. They tasted each other, the tar-like liquor they'd been drinking, and the taste of running fast through the woods so your lungs open up. Then Hayworth jumped down from the rock and ran back through the woods, and she left Flip J. behind.

When she came back to the dead raccoon, Thomas J. sat on the stoop, breathing.

"Where's Flip J?" he asked, "Third place to a seventeen-year-old girl. Too bad."

"He let me win," said Hayworth. She knelt by the raccoon. It looked like it was leaping. Hayworth put her hand into its dull fur. It was still a bit warmer than the air around it. Its black paws were splayed. The bullet had gone in at the shoulder, and the shoulder was torn.

"You're not still upset about that raccoon, are you?" asked Thomas J.

"I'm going to skin it," said Hayworth.

"You don't know how to skin a raccoon."

"Lend me your knife."

Thomas J. came forward unsteadily from all the rum. He gave Hayworth his long knife, which was dull from him practicing throwing it, and it thunking into rotten wood.

Hayworth hefted the raccoon by its tail, but it was heavier than she'd expected, so she sank it back down into the intersection. Its head fell back, its mouth came open, and its teeth were a snarl of needles, useless. Hayworth turned the raccoon on its back. It was a boy raccoon. What Thomas J. had said was true. She didn't know how to skin it. She had never even considered skinning anything in the city that they came from.

Hayworth began between the hind legs with the knife. The blade punctured through the fur and skin easily, slishing inside, but when she turned the blade to pull it upwards towards the chin, she had to use all her strength, she had to use the knife like a saw, and the flesh and fur became ragged. Hayworth opened the raccoon. The stomach slid out onto the ground, a gummy pink sack, dragging a soft heap of intestines. The liver was blue. The kidneys, one after the other, Hayworth held in her hand. Each part was perfect, intact, a neat slick collection, tucked away.

She began to relish the searching knife, the gooey ordered work of it, she cut all the way up to the neck. Hayworth filled her hands with the fur, deep, filthy, and soft, with the layer of long hair skimming over the top, coarse and black tipped. At first the pelt peeled easily back, falling in a heavy fluid fold, but working the skin away from the leg bones stopped her. She had to scrape and scrape with the knife, but still the legs held steadily to their scraps of fur. Hayworth began to feel the night's heat. It started to stink a bit. Hair caked the dull knife.

Thomas J. sat on the storefront steps and sipped rum and water, watching and then not watching Hayworth's progress.

"I don't care about this," he told her. "I don't want to know anything about this. I think we should leave it alone."

"Do we have any salt?" she asked him.

"Salt?"

"I think I should pack the pelt in salt to cure it. Look in the five and dime and see if there's salt."

"I don't want to go in that five and dime all alone without a light," said Thomas J. "Where's Flip J, anyway?"

"I'd have expected him back by now," said Hayworth, looking into the woods.

"I don't like to go around in the dark alone," said Thomas J. "I wish Flip J. would come back."

But Flip J. had left the path to cut through the ash wood, and he caught his foot on a root, and he fell down and hit his head, and he had a long dream, and when he woke up, the moon shone through the trees just like milky daytime. Flip J. turned his head and came nose to nose with a doe's skull, its empty eyes wide with sympathy. He drew himself up to one elbow until he could see that he lay in a dark valley full of tumbling brown leaves. He wasn't lying on any actual ground, just on those shifting leaves, and bumping up underneath the heaps of leaves were skulls, deer skulls, piles of them. They emerged from beneath the valley as if washed to shore. The spindly wood was silent, and it let go a prickly sweet smell that ran all through Flip J. He put his head back down and looked up through the trees at the bright sky. He thought of kissing Hayworth, of how soft-hearted and smart-alecky she was. That's what we think he thought of. That's what we would have been thinking if we had been Flip J, but he was inscrutable and content.

Hayworth left the raccoon and came to sit with Thomas J.

"Wasn't he right behind you?" asked Thomas J, looking hard at her.

"If he's not back soon, we'll go find him," said Hayworth. She put her sticky hand on Thomas J's shoulder.

They waited in the dark on the stoop. A scavenger, a dark animal came sniffing into the intersection towards the raccoon carcass. It was another raccoon. It snuffled and nibbled at the dead raccoon.

"We'll wait for one more minute, and then we'll go look for him," said Hayworth.

"I don't like going around in the dark without him, that's all," said Thomas J.

They waited and waited for Flip J, who'd had a vision. When he came wandering back, blinking into the intersection, they held him and petted him, they clapped him on the back.

THE FISHER CAT

My dad lay in bed looking up at the sloped attic ceiling before he began to drive a garbage truck, then a recycling truck, and of course long before I was born. He lay there, just awake, and he let a fly vomit into his eye. He felt a splash, a small spark of wet. He blinked. All around him, there was stillness, there were socks, there was a Mounds bar, there was a heap of outdated magazines, there was a Swiss army knife. This was his room, he paid good money for it each month, and he built small fires in the fireplace up at the top of the house near where the chimney let out, but above him, in the slope, he was watched.

But so what, each moment was precious to him, who cares, he was lonely, what are you going to do about it, my dad needed a job if he ever wanted to leave that town, so he put on a suit, and he walked down three flights of stairs and out of the house. He walked towards the center of town, wondering, Do I look good in a suit? I wish I had been born yet to tell him, You look good in a suit, Dad. You look good. You're tall and freckled, and you are flabby. You are fit, yet you have never had any real muscle, and neither has anyone I love.

My dad stepped into the intersection where Monroe meets Mudd, he stood on a white painted stripe with his shabby wing-tipped shoes, he walked forward to find a job. A silver Ford sedan inched all the way into the cross-walk, it honked, it jolted, its engine revved. My dad, after a life spent throwing forks at the thought of the silent majority, felt his spine full of shards, felt it right up against his fault line. He raised his noodley arm, and he brought his fist down on the hood of the sedan, and the driver got out of the car and punched my dad in the face, and my dad fell down.

This was in Rock Springs, Wyoming, where the ste-reotype that the rest of the country had was that people there felt bad, and it was true. They felt angry. There was poison around, and a long low plain, and the water was yellow tasting, though it ran clear. My dad did not raise me in Rock Springs, Wyoming. It was bitter there, a blank coldness with no beauty to it. The one restaurant, Meri-weather's, kept the bar shelaqued almost an inch above its actual wood surface, kept a wagon wheel on the wall, a moose head, a bear head, a bobcat head, Indians came in, white people came in.

The man who punched my dad's name was James AuCoin, and he had returned from Vietnam two years previous. He wore a ginger mustache and had the kind of weathering in his face that gave him a constantly reckoning manner. He was handsomer than my dad. He was red, always. After he punched my dad, he did not get back into his car. He left his sedan in the intersection. A slow day, he stepped over my dad, who was unconscious, and he strode across to Meriweather's. Inside, he took a stool, and he put his boots up on the rail beneath the bar. He ordered an Olympia, he lit a cigarette, and he waited.

I hate this man, this James AuCoin. He punched my dad.

Yet, later I would also punch my dad. I would see him cry. I would love him a little less. You could spend your life comforting your dad, but you should not.

Still, I hate James AuCoin, there's no other way. I want to fucking kill him, he decked my jello-legged dad, my man with ideals, my dad's dough ball face pale beneath persistent freckles, punched out. But James AuCoin was trying to make sense of his life, and we are all of us watched, or wish we were. Before he punched my dad, or rather, before my dad thumped the hood of his car, James AuCoin had not felt watched. He had felt distinctly un-scrutinized, so that when he went to the grocery store, no one scolded him for buying only frozen shrimp, though he was on government assistance. No one asked to see his identification. James AuCoin's wife had not been waiting for him when he returned from Vietnam. In fact, she had taken their two children and moved to Laramie.

The bartender slid over an Olympia, and said, "Haven't seen you in a while, Jimmy. Thought you'd left town. Look at you, Jimmy. You're an eyesore."

"Les," said James AuCoin, waiting for my dad, "do you think people can be happy in Rock Springs?"

"Happy? Why are you talking about happy?" asked Les.

"Alright, Les, what would you rather talk about?" said James AuCoin. He pulled the tab on his Olympia, hiss.

"I got a pet. I don't know how to care for it," said Les.

Out in the street, my dad lay unconscious. In his mind, there was a fur covered screen, and when he pushed in on it, a thick imprint in wet sand. My dad felt this pliant, juice-squeezed brain feeling, and then he opened his eyes. He got to his feet. He dusted himself off. His suit jacket had a hole in the elbow. My dad touched his face, and felt tenderness, and felt the color blue. A woman who had watched the whole thing was Judy Cuthbert, who had lived in Rock Springs all her long life, and remembered signs on business doors that said, "No Indians." Pointing, she said, "He went over to Meriweather's." People hoped that the connection to Lewis and Clark would do the town some good, but it did not. It was fabricated.

James AuCoin sat on his barstool, his second Olympia in hand, when my dad walked in.

"Why did you punch me?" my dad asked.

"Are you calling me a son of a bitch?" James AuCoin said.

"Why did you punch me you son of a bitch?" my dad asked.

"What are you going to do about it?" said James Au-Coin. "No one saw it happen. I'm not what you call watched."

"You son of a bitch," my dad said. "Of course you're watched. I'm watched. Everyone's watched."

"Is that right? And how are you watched?' asked James AuCoin.

"This morning, a fly vomited into my eye," said my dad. "I thought I was alone, but there's always someone."

"Not for me, there's not," said James AuCoin. "For me, there's no one. Sometimes three days pass, and I have not had one single conversation."

When you see your dad cry, you love him a little less. For example, at a time in my life when I was an adult, a grown woman, with breasts that shrank a bit every year, firmed up, became less sexy and more utilitarian, my nipples turned white and just stood there, I went to a remote venue for dancing, and I saw a man there that I saw every day. I saw him walking past my house each morning, carrying a Styrofoam cup of coffee, and chewing on his lip. He was a small business owner, almost as if no one had bothered to tell him that would make him miserable. At this remote venue, I watched the man dance, joyous and exuberant, feeling that for once he was not watched. And watching this man dance was like watching my dad cry.

"Do you live here in Rock Springs?" James AuCoin asked, "Because I haven't seen you before."

"I'm new in town," said my dad.

"Why do you live here?" asked James AuCoin.

"My car broke down on the way to Minneapolis. I didn't have the money to get the fan belt fixed, and the person who towed my car thought I was a sissy, because of my tight jeans. But I was in a rock and roll band, where I came from."

"So what?" said James AuCoin.

"We had a regular gig, at a bar in Portland," said my dad.

"Never even heard of it," said James AuCoin.

"I ended up just staying. That was last May. I've been working on and off. I'm still looking for something. But now the day is ruined."

"What, thanks to me?"

"Thanks to you. I haven't seen you around, either, come to think of it."

"No one has," said James AuCoin.

Les, the bartender came over and asked my dad what's yours.

"I'll have what he's having," said my dad.

Les slid over another Olympia. "You look like hell," he said, touching his own eye in sympathy with my dad's shiner.

"Thanks to this jackass," said my dad, "In fact, put this one on his tab,"

"Like hell," said James AuCoin. "What about you, Les? Why do you live here?"

"My car broke down and I never left," said Les.

"I was just saying—" said my dad.

"Les here has got a pet he doesn't know how to care for," said James AuCoin.

"No one knows I have it. Not my wife. No one," said Les.

"Then why are you telling us of all people?" asked James AuCoin.

"What kind of pet?" asked my dad.

"You think I know? I don't know," said Les.

"How can you not know what kind of pet you have?" asked my dad.

"I think it's a fisher cat, because of its bad hyena face. I think it's sick. It's in a pen out behind my shed, and it tries to bite me every day. It's my pet because it stalked me, but then I trapped it before it could hurt me," said Les.

"What do you feed it?" asked my dad.

"I don't know what to feed it," said Les, "so I haven't fed it yet."

"That's bad," said my dad.

"Les, that's very bad," said James AuCoin.

"I think it's a fisher cat," said Les. "Animals everywhere are acting upon us. This one too."

"Acting upon us. Yes," said my dad.

"A fly vomited into this guy's eye, believe it or not," said James AuCoin.

"A fly isn't an animal," said Les.

"Have you ever been punched before?" asked James AuCoin.

"Who are you asking?" asked Les.

"He's asking me," said my dad. "No."

"Fuckin A," said James AuCoin.

"Jimmy, I'm off soon. You want to come over and see the fisher cat?" asked Les. James AuCoin's heart beat and beat.

There would come a time when my dad would stand under a fir tree, and a raccoon would pee on his head. He would look up to see the malicious pointy face looking back at him in triumph.

At seventeen, I kissed a hiker before his hike, I kissed him with tongue, he told me he didn't like having his lower lip licked. In the middle of the night, he woke up and punched a skunk.

Also, a squirrel fell from a tree, and ricocheted off the head of my first husband, as he left me. The squirrel made a noise from deep within, the noise a bird makes if you squeeze it too tightly, a low-toned warm squeak. Then it made for the nearest telephone pole.

The question remains, if jails should even exist, does a person, a searching person like James AuCoin belong in one? He didn't know how to care for anything, never had, that was part of his trouble. With balletic precision, James AuCoin stretched his leg out, and touched his boot to the back of my dad's knee, and my dad's knee collapsed, and my dad spilled his beer.

"You jackass," said my dad, "I'm going to press charges. Les, bring me the phone."

"There's a payphone outside on the corner, sir." said Les.

"This fucking town," said my dad. James AuCoin rose to his feet, swaying just a little. He straightened so that his spine rippled up, cracking, and he stretched to one side, and then the other. He took my dad's shoulder, and he looked my dad level in the eye. My dad took one step backwards, but James AuCoin wound back his other arm, and cut his fist swift up beneath my dad's jaw, so that my dad's head snapped back, and my dad felt, acutely, each one of his teeth, their numbers and positions, then he was on the floor. There was a catch in his throat, a blank spot moving through him, his very tongue breathed.

When my dad woke up the second time, James AuCoin was gone, and Les hoisted him to his feet, helped him to the door, pointed him back towards the intersection of Monroe and Mudd. My dad expected to hear no sound, and he heard no sound. Sounds had to come back to him as he walked away from Meriweather's. Sounds had to come back to him one by one. A horn, a chugging, a cloud sound, a yowl, a bird rumbling over, a whirring, a resonance beneath the sidewalk, a burr, a ping, a sustained round note, Judy Cuthbert still stood on the street next to James AuCoin's sedan.

"He left his car," she said. "Who's going to move this car?"

"I'll move it," said my dad. He walked around to the driver's side of the silver Ford, slow, one wing-tipped shoe after the other, like an old man. He opened the door, and lowered himself down behind the steering wheel. The seats were nests for mice, pulled-up stuffing, ripped leather. The key was in the ignition. Judy Cuthbert walked over to the driver's side window, made the motion of roll your window down. My dad did, leaned out.

"I remember Jimmy when he was a tyke," she said.

"A tyke?" My dad asked.

"He built Rock Spring's first P.A. system. He invented it, while other young men in other places also invented other P.A.'s. Jimmy charged everyone fifty cents to watch movies in the park. He was ten, but look at him. He's not ten anymore. He's nowhere now."

"Did you see where he went?"

"I've been very happy here," said Judy Cuthbert, "but that's not saying a lot. I just watch what goes on, and the sky, and the plains, and the mountains. All these loping cats."

"Do you have a family?" asked my dad.

"Of course I do," said Judy Cuthbert. "You're new. You go home, and get cleaned up. Pack sugar into those wounds." She stood away from the car, waved him past. He started up the sedan, and rolled.

My dad looked at his face in the rearview mirror. His chin was a mass of yellow and blue and red, and his eye was swollen shut. There was blood on his suit. His suit was torn, and his elbow, poking through, was swollen. His wrist ached where he had caught himself falling. His neck felt like it sat in a cage, he smarted and stung. My dad drove James AuCoin's car the two blocks back to his own house, parked, and hefted himself out, crick by crick.

My dad stood on the front walk, and came then to the point in his life where he could not bring himself to move one more step. He could not picture spending all day stinging in his attic, his face a mash. He could not read one more outdated magazine. Not *Mad*, not *Cracked*, not *Penthouse*, not *Popular Mechanics*, not *Creem*, not *Crawdaddy*, not *National Lampoon*. His Mounds bar was stale. He did not have any sugar to pack into his wounds. My dad stood on his front walk, and began to twitch towards tears. He heaved air deeply into himself to stop this process from happening. I was not born yet, was being prepared somewhere not even sleeping, but the process that would make my dad alien to me began here. We would come together always over business. We would hammer out details. Strategies would include pouring water right down our throats, excusing ourselves, fixing it, I would become expert in tenderness towards him, him helpless, me true.

My dad's landlady pushed open the screen door, and came out onto the front porch. She was in her ninth month of pregnancy, and she wore a tight red dress of some knitted cloth. My dad's relationship to her had previously been one only of rent checks in the mailbox, and once he had traveled through her apartment to the fuse box, where he flipped a circuit- breaker. Now, her face had gone to double chinned rosiness. Her body had become a series of globes. Her breasts, buns, and belly all strained against the forgiving bright fabric she had chosen. Darkened spots appeared all over this gown, spots of spreading moisture, like pie crusts being rolled out. She had a long ponytail, and a nose my dad had previously wanted to press down on with his thumb. Right now, her smell, all the way from the front porch, was one hundred percent soda and yeast. She surveyed my dad.

"What happened to you?" she asked.

"I got punched in the face twice. I got knocked out," said my dad, heaving.

"Why are you driving Jimmy AuCoin's Ford?" said his landlady.

"I'm driving the car of the man who punched me in the face," said my dad.

"I thought he'd left town."

"No, he's still here," said my dad.

"Did you fight back?" asked his landlady. My dad stood in place. His landlady took her hair elastic out, then re-did her ponytail with a snap. She burped. "Excuse me," she said. Underneath her arms, dark wetness steamed. She scratched her left nipple.

"Can I borrow some sugar?" asked my dad.

She opened her screen door and he followed her inside the house. He followed her rump, one-two into the kitchen, and she sat him down in a kitchen chair. "It's a special day for me," she said from the pantry.

"What day is it?" asked my dad.

"It's my due date," she said.

"Congratulations," said my dad. He raised his arms and put his hands out, open, then moved them back to his sides, but she wasn't in the room to see him do this. She returned with the sugar. At the sink, she ran hot water, wet a kitchen rag with hot water. She splashed vinegar onto it, then pulled a chair to face my dad. She sat down, planted one thick leg on either side of my dad's knees, and leaned towards him, reaching up with the cloth. His knees pushed into her skirt, folded it towards where the baby was scheduled to come out that day. She smelled like the forest floor and cheese.

"Hold still," she said. My dad breathed through his nose, fast. Some snot flew out and onto his landlady.

"Breathe slowly," she said.

"Thank you," he said. She cleaned the wound on his chin and underneath his eye. Then she began to press and pat sugar into each place.

"Son of a bitch," said my dad, "Sorry."

"It's making this weird sort of blood jelly," she said, and began to laugh. "Why don't you stay for dinner tonight?" she asked.

"Tonight?"

"Yes, I'll grill. I'll make banana bread. I'll make pie."

"But what if you have your baby? Today? Tonight?" my dad asked. He had misgivings. My dad had thrown many forks, he had acted out many times on principle. When I would grow to punch my dad, I would have misgivings of my own. But dads have lived for so long, hiding bicycles in garages to teach their young families lessons about responsibility, and avoiding small children who aren't their own small children, not knowing what to say to them. My dad thought that it was unreasonable for his landlady to invite him to dinner on the day that she was scheduled to give birth, but he wasn't sure, because he was inexperienced.

He relied on more experienced people to make the correct decisions about childbearing, and about landlord- tenant relationships. He did not like to be implicated in something he felt might be out of his control, but he was not certain how to communicate this. Yet, if dads cannot be certain, who, I ask, can we expect certainty from?

"We'll eat early, just in case," she said.

"Well, if you're sure," he said.

"What's this in your eye?" she asked, "a little mud spot? Does it feel like anything?"

"That's vomit," my dad said. "This morning a fly vomited into my eye."

"That's happened to me before," she said, "You just sit here. Blink a lot. If that doesn't work, we'll try something else."

"Thank you," my dad said again. He blinked rapidly, and like a slide show she moved through her kitchen. She dripped fat into cast-iron, she cut cold butter into flour, she thawed frozen berries, she patted flour and pepper into meat, she browned meat in a skillet, she mashed bananas with a fork, she spooned the pulp into a glass bowl. "Grease this pan," she told my dad, and he did that.

She washed her hands, packed more sugar onto my dad's face, then washed her hands again. She served him a bloody cut of meat. She served him banana bread. He stayed for pie. It was only five o'clock.

Over coffee, she said, "I forgot to ask if you're allergic to anything."

"It's fine, because there is no recorded case of a human being having an allergic reaction to meat. It's scientifically impossible, I think," said my dad.

"But you could be allergic to bananas."

"I'm not, don't worry," said my dad.

"But you could be allergic to bread. Well, to flour. To flour, or yeast, or tree nuts, or sugar or salt," she said.

"Human beings can't be allergic to salt, scientifically, or at least there are no recorded cases that I know of," said my dad.

"But you could be allergic to butter, or berries, or apples, or cinnamon. Or raisins. Lemon juice. Vanilla."

"I'm not, though, don't worry," said my dad.

"But I should have asked, and I'm sorry," said his landlady.

"Don't be," said my dad.

"A fly vomits into your eye in preparation for where it will lay its eggs," she said.

"No, please," said my dad, "that's disgusting."

"It's true," she said.

"Can I ask you something?" asked my dad.

"Okay," she said.

"Is that milk you're leaking?"

"No," she said, "It's something else."

"What is it?" asked my dad.

"It's what comes before milk," she said, "it's like apple juice but it doesn't smell or act like apple juice."

"To me it looks like milk," said my dad.

"It's colostrum," said his landlady.

"Are you afraid of having a baby?" asked my dad.

"Yes," said his landlady, "I can't help it."

Her yeast and moss smell came at him. The colostrum leaking onto her dress pooled in her bellybutton, clotted there, and became cheese. My dad experienced a leap of his insides towards his young landlady, her yeast and soda, her mushroom scent, her damp neck and upper chest, her damp everywhere, the hairs on her. He wondered when he would finally meet my mom. Soon, my dad realized, there would be milk, and he wanted to be near milk like this milk more, to be near milk like this milk, as near as he could get, to smell it, and to help manage it in some way. But he had not met my mom yet, or any woman he felt very strongly about. If I had been born and in conversation with my dad at a time like this, I would have been firm with him. I would have told him, I meet one person after another that I feel strongly about. They come rushing at me, bombarding me, and I'm not saying I like it. His eyes welled up, like mine do now.

"I have to go up to my attic now," he said.

"Please stay," she said. "I might need your help."

"No, I can't," he said, "I'm sorry. I don't know what to do. Don't you have anyone else?"

"No," she said.

"But what were you planning on doing if I hadn't got punched in the face today?" asked my dad.

"I was planning on doing it myself, but now that you're here, I can't imagine being alone anymore," she said.

"No," my dad said, "I'm not ready yet. I'm sorry."

Stricken, he left her sitting at the kitchen table, and he went up to the attic, and soon after that she went into labor. My dad sat in his attic, and built a small fire, and stared at the grate, an issue of *National Lampoon* open on his lap. He prodded his wounds, and felt the sugar blood jelly. Then he stopped doing that. He heaved breaths. He heard heaving breaths. He heard running feet. He heard grunts and a growl like someone had been socked. He heard his landlady yelling, "You smell bad. You stink. Bastard. Bitch. Son of a—" He heard feet on the attic stairs. She knocked on the door to the attic. My dad went down and stood by the door and said, "Who is it?"

The landlady said, "I need your help."

My dad said, "I cannot help you with this. I can't help, I can't, I can't, I can't, I can't, I can't, I can't, I can't. I'm sorry, I'm sorry, I'm sorry, I'm sorry, I'm sorry."

"You have to," she said. "You have to."

"I can't."

"Please drive me to the hospital," she said, "There's no one else."

"I don't have a car," he said. But then he remembered that he did have a car.

My dad is not an artist, an inventor, a motorcyclist, a mechanic, a cook, a spy, a carpenter, a sign maker, or a boat builder. In many ways, he is just a dad. He goes through life making lists, listing me, loving me. My life with him has been a business meeting and something else. My dad once told me what a fisher cat was. A fisher cat, my dad told me, is bigger than an otter, but not as ugly as a wolverine. A fisher cat does not fish. Its mouth is round like a shark's mouth. If a fisher cat attacks a person, my dad said, it is probably dead by now, because it was probably sick to begin with.

My dad has given me gifts, complete sets of handsome brown books, weeks of sailing lessons, black and white movies, records full of music that I am singing as I write. I have accepted these gifts and torn through them, tried to love them the way he loves them, to experience my dad's life before I was there to watch him. You could spend your life trying to experience this, but you should not. My dad is helpless in his mystery. He is a mystery to me. His plan is to force me, in the future, to live long years without him, just as he lived so long without me. For this, I will never forgive him.

My dad opened the door to his attic, and took his young landlady in his arms. "Breathe," he said to her.

"I know," she said, "I know better than you do."

"I'm only trying to help," he said.

"I know," she said, "Thank you."

My dad bundled his young landlady into James Au-Coin's car, and he drove her to the hospital. She lay across the back seat making a racket, reaching up to punch my dad on the shoulder with great strength. "I'm sorry," she gasped, "but it makes me feel better."

"I know it does," said my dad. She soaked the back seat.

My dad waited at the hospital all night. He slept on a bench made from four hard yellow chairs pushed together. At three o'clock in the morning, he woke up, his face stinging. The lights were still bright, people padded by in thick white shoes, a low table held *Highlights: Fun with a Purpose*, *Woman's Day*, and *Family Circle*. My dad fished a ballpoint pen from his breast pocket. He opened *Highlights*, and began to write in the margins, in the blank spaces at the ends of paragraphs, and on all the activity pages meant for mazes. He wrote all over Goofus and Gallant, between the lines of the Timber Toes, and around the edges of a story about a cat who went up in a hot air balloon. First he made a list of each person he had ever known, and next he made a list with my name right at the top. It was a list of each person that he hoped, one day, to meet.

PLANET X

The Bells went to the ocean but it was too loud and big, like usual. They sat nearby, over a rise, on the bank of a creek with sand, not even real sand, but pebbly, wormy sand, with fleas. The worst thing, Cora Bell thought, is how they avoided eye contact with me in the car when they played that awful game about the space capsule leaving Earth. The space capsule leaves, and only a few people can go along, and the rest of the people are left to die. The rules, for God's sake, state that when you kill off a member of the Earth community, you have to make eye contact with them when you say, "You die." It's part of the moral point the game is trying to make. You have to look the person in the face, and say, "You are expendable, Cora Bell. You are old, and let's face it, what do you do anymore but crosswords all day." But they had not made eye contact with her. They had put an end to the game rather than admit she would be the one to be left behind.

Cora's son, Chuck Bell, heaved over onto his side to listen to the radio.

"Cleveland's winning," he said. Audrey Bell, Cora's daughter in-law, struggled to put sun lotion on Eugene Bell, who was eight. Eugene squirmed free, and ran down the bank into the water.

"Eugene, your aqua socks," said Audrey.

"I don't want my stupid aqua socks," said Eugene.

"It's dangerous to be barefoot," said Audrey.

"So what? Who cares? Right, Grandma? Who cares?"

"You stay out of this," Audrey told Cora. Then to Eugene, "Listen, Eugene, there are certain people who think it's all right to pee in rivers, and they contaminate the water for all the rest of us. You can get worms that burrow into the bottoms of your feet, is what I'm saying."

"Worms! Worms!" said Eugene, and hopped around.

"Why don't you work on the story you're writing instead of playing in the water?"

"I was going to anyway, not because you told me to," said Eugene, and came up the bank. He went to his knapsack, and took out a pocket sized lab notebook with a ballpoint pen clipped to it. He took out a pair of red sunglasses, shaped like stars. He put them on. He sat on a piece of driftwood, with his face screwed up and his tongue sticking out one side of mouth. Every minute or so, he scribbled a few words before flipping the page rapidly. The second worst thing, thought Cora, is how my son has turned into an enormous man, covered with moles and a truly unusual amount of hair. Also, he has married an enormous woman with a tiny head. It struck her anew, though she had known it for a long time.

"Dad?" said Eugene.

"What?" Chuck rolled his head over towards Eugene. The sand fleas hopped.

Chuck turned the radio off. "I said, what is it, Eugene?" Eugene rubbed his nose and frowned. "I love you," he said.

"That's what he always says when he forgets what he was going to say," Chuck said. He rolled back over.

"You used to do that," Cora told Chuck.

"Mother," he said, "Please. I didn't." He flipped the game back on. Cora looked at Eugene. "He did," she said.

"Want to hear my story, Grandma?" asked Eugene. The third worst thing, Cora thought, is how Audrey had insisted they lock the dog in the car all day because of its tendency to drink saltwater. "I'd love to hear your story, Eugene," Cora said. She went to sit next to him on the driftwood. Eugene flipped back to the beginning of his notebook. "I met him at the candy store. He turned around and smiled at me," he began. He looked at Cora, "You get the picture?" Without thinking, Cora responded, "Yes, we see." Audrey said, "Eugene, nobody likes a plagiarist." To Cora, she said, "He's been working on that story for days. Nothing we say seems to matter. But at least it keeps him out of trouble, right?"

"That's how I fell for The Leader of the Pack," Eugene went on.

"Vroom, vroom," helped Cora, confused.

"It's because he has no imagination," said Chuck. "He got my genes, no imagination, nothing up there. Serious, you tell the kid to draw a picture, he'll just sit there looking at you. Doesn't know what to draw. Serious. My genes."

"I imagine lots of stuff," Eugene said, putting his notebook down, "I imagine getting stabbed right in the eyeball." He blinked rapidly. He fell back into the sand.

"Let's eat the sandwiches now," said Audrey. She sat forward and passed the lunch pack around. The sandwiches were sweaty yellow cheese and mayonnaise like pus. The fourth worst thing, thought Cora, is this.

"I want to go to the beach," Cora said, "I thought we came here to go to the beach."

"It's loud," said Audrey, "but you can go on over if you want."

"Eugene, let's go to the beach," said Cora. "You can play in the ocean."

"Sit up and eat your sandwich first, Eugene," said Audrey. Eugene sat up. He took the sandwich his mother held out for him. He slithered the cheese onto his tongue. "This tastes like saliva," said Eugene.

"If you go to the beach, Cora, just make sure to listen for the mooing," said Audrey.

"What mooing?" asked Cora. She set her sandwich underneath the driftwood, and scooped a little pebbly, wormy sand over it.

"If a tidal wave is coming they've got this siren that sounds like mooing."

"It means you've got to get in your car and drive like hell," said Chuck.

"Okay," said Cora, "alright. Let's go, Eugene."

"What makes a tidal wave?" asked Eugene.

"An earthquake," said Chuck.

"What makes an earthquake?" asked Eugene.

"A comet hitting the earth," said Cora.

"Actually, I think you mean meteor," said Chuck.

"Oh please. That is so dumb," said Audrey.

"A comet! A comet!" said Eugene. "Dad, is that going to happen?"

"No," said Chuck. He turned the radio up. "Cleveland," he said, "it's their game to lose, I'd say."

"Mom, is that going to happen? Is that comet coming?" asked Eugene. He put down his sandwich.

"No, Eugene."

"They've got missiles," said Chuck, "you know, pointed at outer space."

Cora stood up and took Eugene by the hand.

"Eugene, your aqua socks," said Audrey.

"What a team," said Chuck to the radio, "what a team."

Cora and Eugene walked away. They went over a little rise. Eugene hopped along the pieces of driftwood, and Cora pushed herself among them, using the logs for support. The wind picked up as they came out onto the wide beach, smooth and empty, stretching far away towards the South. The sky was large, vacuuming upwards, white and blue. They walked down to the waves.

"The foam is dead mermaids," said Eugene.

"Why don't you write a story about that?" asked Cora.

"There's already a story about that," said Eugene. He took his red sunglasses shaped like stars out of his pocket. He put them on.

"There's already a story about The Leader of the Pack, too," said Cora.

"There's already all the stories. That's the trouble," said Eugene.

"Eugene, that's not true," said Cora.

"Yes it is, Grandma. Name one."

"Name one what?"

"Name one kind of old days adventure. The old kind of adventures, where they didn't already know how everything was going to turn out."

Cora thought quickly. "What about the pee worms burrowing into your feet?"

"Grandma," said Eugene, "pee doesn't have worms in it."

"The tidal wave, then."

"We'd get in our car and drive like hell. There would be mooing. Trust me, I've already thought about all this."

"Then the comet."

"That doesn't count, either. Remember, the missiles aimed at outer space?" Eugene made swirling holes with his toes, swirling, salty holes that sprung back like bread dough.

"Do you really imagine getting stabbed in the eyeball?" asked Cora.

"Yes."

"Why?"

"I don't know. I guess because it usually makes me feel better."

All at once the sky was full of sea birds, exploded from a haystack rock down the beach, diving and diving, and crying like their hearts would break. Both Cora and Eugene dropped their heads back to look at the wheeling birds. Then Cora was hungry. This was a lot of work. All at once there was nothing more important than getting her grandson that particular bit of information that she had failed, somehow, to get to her leathery, mole covered, thick necked son.

"Eugene," she raised her voice above the sea birds. "There are no missiles."

"There aren't?"

"Probably not."

Eugene brightened. He lifted his sunglasses and squinted at Cora.

"What else?" he asked.

"Lots of things," she said.

"What?" he asked.

"The space capsule," said Cora.

"What about it?"

"I would be expendable. In the space capsule game, I would be the least useful member of the Earth community. I'm old. What do I do anymore but crosswords all day?"

Eugene looked at the sand, embarrassed. "Oh, Grandma, the space capsule is just a stupid game."

"Maybe. But it's true that there are places where the old people go and sit by the river with only a blanket, no food or water. They sit by the river and wait to die, and then their bodies roll down into the water and they're carried away."

"Why would they do that?"

"Think about it, Eugene. When there's not enough food, they sacrifice themselves for the younger ones. They know when their time's up."

"Their bodies roll down into the creek?"

"They're washed out to sea." Cora looked at Eugene.

"Sea foam," he said, staring at the sand. "Sea foam."

"Are you hungry?" asked Cora.

"Not those Saliva-wiches, please."

"Let's harvest mussels."

"I've never done that."

"Neither have I."

Cora started off across the sand towards the rock the sea birds had exploded from. Eugene stuffed his sunglasses in his pocket and hurried after her. They would have to wade out to the rock, but only a short way through the tide. Cora plunged in. The sharp cold filling her canvas shoes made the rest of her feel warm for a minute. Eugene hopped along behind her. She grew more determined.

"Have you heard of red tide, Eugene?"

"What's that? Is it blood?"

"It's a poison that lives in shellfish."

"Do you die?"

"Yes."

"How?"

"You get a disease that makes you stay awake forever." They reached the rock, and Cora pulled herself up onto it, then sat with her hands on her knees, breathing. When she thought about it, she decided that the staying awake until you die disease was probably from cannibalism, not red tide, but she wasn't about to turn back. Eugene scrambled up beside her. "Why does staying awake make you die?" he asked.

"During the day, your spine loses its fluid. It takes all night while you sleep to fill it back up."

"And you need that spinal fluid to stay alive?" asked Eugene.

"Right."

"There's probably a cure," said Eugene, looking sideways at Cora.

"There is no cure," said Cora. The sea birds had flown away, but the wind was louder now. She didn't see any mussels.

"Come on, Eugene. There are only barnacles here. We've got to climb around to the other side. You won't cut your feet, will you?"

"No," said Eugene. Slowly, they made their way around the rock, leaning into it with their bodies. "It would be better if we had tentacles," observed Eugene, but Cora was too out of breath to answer. The other side of the rock was more sheltered, and she rested some more. Eugene sat a little apart, watching her.

"Are you going to have a heart attack?" he asked her.

"No, not right now," she said. "We didn't bring any water, did we?"

"I could spit into your mouth," he said, "I could cut open my arm and you could drink my blood, I saw it once."

"Please don't spit into my mouth. I'll be fine," she said.

"Do you want to go back?" he asked after a moment. He took his sunglasses out of his pocket and raised them to his face.

"No," said Cora, getting to her feet. "No, we came her to get mussels." She looked around. The waves sprayed up a little closer, and the sea birds flew closer again, in their loyal, warring family. Out on the horizon, she saw another haystack rock the mirror of their own, but she could see the breakers hard against it, suspended high like exclamation points. The battering ocean threw salt in her eyes, but down at her feet she caught a glimpse of blue beneath seaweed. "There," she said, but she would have to climb down to them. "Help me down to those, Eugene." She pointed, and Eugene came forward, and took one of her arms. Heavily, Cora lowered herself down the rock. Then she leaned her body back into it, and reached out for the mussels. "I've got you, Grandma," said Eugene, holding her in the soft scoop of her armpit, where it hurt her. She grabbed hold of one of the blue shells and pulled hard, but the mussel didn't budge. Cora paused, and wiped hair out of her eyes. Her hand shook. "Goddammit," she said, "Goddammit." She felt her face go red. Eugene tightened his grip. "Grandma, we could just have sandwiches," he said.

"No," she said, "Goddammit, no. Now just hold on a minute." Cora tugged at the mussel again, pressing herself back into Eugene's grip. She gritted her teeth and pulled. Eugene leaned forward, holding her, and his sunglasses slid out of his pocket, and went skidding down the rock into the ocean. Eugene threw his weight back against the rock. Cora slipped. She plunged her hand down into the mussel bed, and felt her skin rip open rudely. Cora skidded down the rock face, so that one foot hit the breakers before she caught herself. The rough salt water was cold enough to burn. Above her, Eugene's shocked face was white and red. Below her, his red sunglasses, star shaped, tossed against and against the rock on top of the foam. She steadied herself, breathing unevenly. "Are you alright, Eugene?" Cora called up to him.

"Your hand's bleeding, Grandma."

"I see your glasses. I'm going down for them."

"Grandma, I think you should come back up now. I think we should go back."

"Just hold on. I'll get your glasses." The steady ocean roar was the sound of an echo again and again, overlapping. The sea birds were a family, diving to the beach. One of them fell nearby, and didn't move. Cora's hand lay open on the black rock, gaping with blood. Eugene opened his mouth and screamed.

Eugene screamed with his hands by his side and his head back. His mouth was stretched deep and black, missing a few teeth. His body sank back into the rock. Drowning out the ocean and the sea birds, he screamed and screamed and screamed for a long time.

Cora left the mussels and the sunglasses, and climbed up the rock to him. She took him by the arm, and gently turned him towards the shore. Eugene screamed as he had when he'd been a baby, with abandon and strangely clear eyes. Even as he screamed, he climbed carefully along next to Cora, until they were able to climb back down into where the waves swam into the beach. The tide had come in some, and the water was up to Eugene's knees, pulling at his skinny legs. Cora kept hold of his arm, and pulled harder the other way. One of her canvas shoes stuck deep in the sand, and the ocean sucked it off her foot. She kept walking. She walked with Eugene back to shore, and he screamed all the way up to the dry sand. His bare feet were white and pink, the toenails rough and round. She sat him down on a piece of driftwood. "Stop screaming," she said. Eugene gulped once and was still.

When he spoke, his voice was clear. "I don't care about any space capsule. I won't let you go to the river without me." They sat side by side. It was late afternoon.

When Eugene and Cora got back to the creek, Chuck and Audrey lay interchangeably side by side.

"Aud pulled a tick out of my armpit while you were gone. This big. Serious," said Chuck.

"I just leaned forward and pulled it right out," said Audrey. "I said, 'Chuck, honey, don't move an inch,' and then I just… well, you know the rest."

"She did," said Chuck.

"Ticks can cause major personality changes," Cora said.

"Audrey pulled it out," Chuck said.

"Even if they're only in there for a minute, they can cause personality changes," Cora said, "something you might not even notice."

"Oh, I noticed all right," said Audrey. "It's been hell."

Chuck switched on the radio. Cleveland was still winning. "Cleveland's still winning," said Chuck. Audrey sat forward and moved her tongue all around her mouth, then spat out some crumbs from the sandwich.

"Hey, what's the big idea?" asked Chuck. He rapped on the radio, "What happened to my game?" It had gone to snow.

"Cora, look at your hand. It's bleeding," said Audrey.

"We tried to get mussels," said Eugene, "but we didn't want to stay awake until we died."

"Cora, where's your shoe?" asked Audrey.

"It's just a scrape," said Cora.

"I've got band aids. You know people pee in the ocean. You don't want to get worms," said Audrey.

"Our spines need fluid," said Eugene, "warm thick spine fluid."

"My game," said Chuck. The snow cleared and the radio was silent. Then an announcer's voice cut in. "Citizens," the announcer said. "This is an official national broadcast. Citizens, we are in a state of emergency. We have just received word from NASA that a comet approximately two miles in diameter is headed for our planet, and will impact in approximately eight hours. Citizens, it is important that we do not panic. If you're going to go anywhere, Citizens, just probably, go to the country or something. There's really no safe place. But citizens, if I were you, I personally would go someplace beautiful, I guess. I myself am taking my wife to a little orchard outside of Cleveland where we went on our first date. But citizens, you could, I don't know, go to the beach or the woods, or the farm where you were born. Something like that. Might as well. This comet is predicted to have the effect of approximately twenty thousand hydrogen bombs. That's what NASA says. It's not really something I can imagine. Eight hours. Don't panic." Snow cut in, then a recorded voice, "DO NOT PANIC. CITIES ARE BEING EVACUATED. REMEMBER. WE HAVE MISSILES. DO NOT PANIC." More snow.

The Bells sat together and watched the radio. Snow, snow, and snow. They watched the radio. The light faded. The stars came out.

"Who was that, Jimmy Stewart? What is this, Mr. Smith Goes To Washington? This is ridiculous. Let's go home," said Chuck. "What happened to my game, for crying out loud?"

"Yes, let's. I'm hungry and tired," said Audrey. "Eugene, you're hungry and tired."

"I'm not hungry or tired," said Eugene.

"There are no missiles," said Cora firmly. Eugene took her hand.

Back at the car, the dog had wriggled out a back window and escaped. Also, the battery was dead. "I'm not camping out here," said Audrey. "I want to go home. Chuck?"

It was dark, and in the background the ocean continued its racket. Cora opened the trunk, and took out a woolen blanket, and her warm sweater. She found the box of band aids and put it in her pocket. She slipped out of her one canvas shoe, and turned barefoot from the car.

"Some day off this turned out to be," said Chuck. He walked out of the parking area, onto the shoulder of the road. The cars were rushing lights. Audrey followed him. They waved at the lights.

Cora and Eugene walked back to the creek. They went over the rise and picked their way through the shadowy hulks of driftwood. They spread the wool blanket on the beach. Cora put on her sweater. Eugene opened his knapsack and put on a cap. He put on his aqua socks.

"Are you afraid?" asked Cora.

"Yes," said Eugene.

"Me too," said Cora.

"Let's sleep right here on the beach," said Eugene.

"Alright," said Cora. There was a pattering sound, and the dog ran out from the shadows, wild eyed. Eugene held his trembling body until he was still.

The three of them breathed next to each other. The waves sounded closer and then farther away. Somewhere, a sea bird made a settling noise. It was too dark to see the mussel rock. All they could see was the sky. They could see satellites, and the milky way, and the moon. They could see the Big Dipper, and Orion's Belt. They could see stars collapsing. They could see brown dwarves, white dwarves, pulsars, quasars, supernovas, solar flares, nebulas, and red giants. They could see worm holes and the dark side of the moon. They could see Planet X.

When the shooting stars began to fall, Cora folded the blanket over them, tucking her feet warmly inside. Eugene held the dog. His breathing evened into sleep. The shooting stars were warm and stormy all around them, falling to the beach. Cora and Eugene closed their eyes. Their spines filled quietly up with cream and honey.

ACTIVITY SUMMER

Pedaling over to the Eastside, I cut along the ridge where Ulysses Park pitches downwards to Sherman Lake, and there was the Hawaii-Sno-Cone cart, out front of the closed and locked community pool where each summer one person drowns. The Hawaii-Sno-Cone cart, never seen before the hottest late June day, lunged straight up out of the grass. It was March third, low-down ditch cold, with steel skies threatening rain and more. The park was empty of even the most hardy children, the ones who wore Eskimo hoods and chose day by day whether they were a boy or a girl and didn't care who believed them, not mom, not dad, not anyone. Yet there was the Hawaii-Sno-Cone cart, serene, bright, and open for business. I brought my bike up short in surprise. When I circled back, it was Marvin Staples who, for three dollars, sold me a root beer Sno-Cone with black cherry syrup over the top. I chose it because the pink and orange sandwich board out front said it was the daily special. The sandwich board also said, in round hasty letters, "THIS IS THE END."

I had not seen Marvin Staples since we had gone to Ulysses High School together five years earlier, but I guess I knew he was still in the neighborhood. Most of us were still in the neighborhood, the economy being what it was, and our self-esteems so low. I graduated from Columbia Pinnacle Community College with an Associates Degree, one black eye which was not my fault, and Professor Strickland's assurance that I was the next Chuck Norris, and I still think he meant Chuck Palahniuk. He told me that, for a girl, I was able to write stories with quite a lot of shooting off of guns.

For the two years since, I had worked at a Vietnamese restaurant with a banner that I had not deciphered, and at 31 Flavors. They faced each other at either end of a business park one block from Ulysses High. At the Vietnamese place, I sold bowls of the same thing over and over again, but with different names. The Vietnamese gangs came around and shot it up once in while, which made it famous but not at all safe. At 31 Flavors, the Jamocha Almond Fudge could be counted on for freezer burn each day of the year. The manager, pale, splotchy, and just my age, tried in vain to grow a moustache. He took me out once, just once. He never got the monthly 31 Flavors Lip Synch Night off the ground, which might have been easy with an ounce, just one ounce, of self-confidence. But I'm editorializing.

Look, two years out of Columbia Pinnacle, I was still riding my bike to Professor Strickland's apartment on the Eastside after work most days. He maintained he had a lot in store for me. "Like what?" I'd ask in the middle of the clammy night, and he'd say, "world travel, the opera, the theater, anything you want."

"I want to visit the ocean," I'd say, and then I'd wait. Each time, I believed in waiting.

"The ballet, the Rolling Stones, you name it," he continued. In the morning it was cereal again, and not the good kind. He'd shaved off his beard to make himself look younger but all I saw was his wobbly chin. Look, two years out of Columbia Pinnacle, I had never even seen the Pacific.

Marvin Staples had been one year above me at Ulysses High. In high school, he was triumphant. He said frisbee was better than sex, said argyle socks were better than frisbee, he built a new bike out of scrap parts for prom, homecoming, and graduation. He had eyes for everything except for me. Five years post graduation, his hair still rolled down his back.

"One root beer Sno-Cone with black cherry syrup, coming up," he said. "Now, you know this is no substitute for real nutrition, don't you? It's primarily made up of water and sugar, which can only get you so far." He was friendly but I could see that he had not yet focused too much on my face.

"Marvin Staples," I said. "It's been since high school. I didn't know you were still in the neighborhood. And working at the Hawaii-Sno-Cone cart in March. Early March."

"I'm not sure I remember you," said Marvin. The space heater inside the Sno-Cone stand blasted a hot breeze against his body. He had the relaxed skin of a warm person in a cold month. The metal rivets of his jeans glowed. He glanced past my shoulder. "In fact, I'm sure I don't. Did we have a class together? Were you particularly known for anything? In fact, what's your name?"

"It's Yancy," I said.

"Yancy. Nice to meet you again."

"We had health class together my Junior year. Your Senior year."

"Oh yeah?" he said, handing over my Sno-Cone. He checked the clock behind the register. The clock face was the portrait of a smiling Eskimo child with enormous blue eyes. "Aloha!" was written across the child's forehead. I put my tongue to the black cherry syrup. I stood at the Hawaii-Sno-Cone cart window and looked in at Marvin.

"Those were my ugly days," I told him.

He tore his eyes away from the clock. I met his gaze. For a moment, we looked. "Yancy," he said, "Yancy …"

"Yancy Butler," I said, "It's alright. Really. I wasn't very attractive. I expected to look back later and realize I was too hard on myself, but I actually look back now and think I had it just about right. Small, tired eyes, bad skin, and a nose shiny with worry."

"Shiny with worry, is that what it was?" Marvin had a nose, and in fact an entire muzzle, that reminded me of a sympathetic bruin. But now he was gazing past me, and saying, "So who's this? This yours?"

I looked down to see that a small girl in a sea-foam green Eskimo hood had appeared at my right.

"Not mine," I said laughing, trying to grasp at that previous moment. Talking out loud about my unattractiveness had never failed to get me what I wanted. At Columbia Pinnacle, Professor Strickland had listened during his office hours, and complied on his own time.

But the sea-foam-hood child, whose wind-dry red cheeks seemed to be filled with marbles, had arrived quietly and quite alone. Marvin and I gazed into the depths of the park and the locked community pool building until our eyes streamed, but she did not seem to have even one parent or guardian.

"Hey," said Marvin, leaning out of his window to the little girl, "Are you unattended?"

"Where is your mommy?" I asked her. She said nothing, but pointed with one sea-foam green mittened finger towards Sherman Lake.

"Oh, shit," said Marvin.

"Is your mommy coming soon?" I asked.

"She must mean her mommy's in the lake," said Marvin. We looked at the little girl. Her cheeks bulged. She shook her head.

"Where's mommy?" I asked.

"This isn't going anywhere," Marvin said, "She's got something in her mouth. Get that stuff out of her mouth."

"Open your mouth," I said to the girl. She shook her head. I knelt down.

"Would you like some of my Sno-Cone? It's root beer flavored." The kid rolled her eyes.

"Stick your finger in her mouth, that's what you've got to do, trust me," said Marvin.

"Why should I trust you? What do you know about kids?" I turned back to the kid. "Come on. Don't you like black cherry?" Her mouth stayed closed.

"I've got two of them," said Marvin. He gave me this information as if in exchange for his not leaving the heated cart to actually help out. Two kids, and what did I have, right? At that moment, it felt like not much of anything.

"That's what you've been doing since high school? Where are they?" I asked him.

"My girl took them when she left."

"Your girl?"

"My wife, Shoshona. The owner of the whole Hawaii-Sno-Cone operation. She left me with the cart. She's gone for good, I think, so I decided to open it during the off season. What would you have done?" Marvin, who had been looking at me, he really had, now delivered his words only to the sea-foam girl. The metal door to the cart stayed closed, efficiently conducting heat.

"You used to stick your fingers in your kids' mouths?" I asked him. The girl opened her eyes wider.

"It's the only way sometimes. My wife, Shoshona, she tried talking to them in Spanish. She'd say, like, 'Not in *la boca*' but they didn't understand Spanish, so I'd just stick my fingers in their mouths."

The girl began to drool.

"Not in *la boca*," I said. The girl just stared at me. Marvin tapped his fingers impatiently, and made the decision to come out the side door of the Sno-Cone cart. He knelt down in front of the little girl, who did not resist. He held her jaw gently with one hand, and pushed his hooked index finger through her pursed lips. He withdrew a saliva soaked acorn. It slipped from his grasp, bounced once on the ground, and rolled slowly down towards the lake. The kid spit out one acorn after another, until her cheeks were empty. Then she reached out and clamped one of her arms decisively around Marvin's shin. "I'm a squirrel," the girl said.

"What'd I tell you?" asked Marvin, wiping his hand on his pants, "Not in *la boca*. I'm so sure." He patted the girl on the head. She pushed her head up into his hand, turning her hood side to side like a cat being scratched.

"Where's your mommy squirrel?" I asked her.

"Squirrels don't have mommies," she said.

"Cut it out, Yancy," said Marvin. "If there's one thing I hate, it's this indulgent nonsense." He turned to the girl, and asked firmly, his face kind, "How old are you?"

"I'm six," said the girl, "I'm in kindergarten."

"What's your name, little squirrel?" I asked.

"Squirrels don't have names." She frowned at me, and burrowed her head into the back of Marvin's knee. She wouldn't let go of him.

"I said knock it off, Yancy. This is the last thing we need," said Marvin, keeping his hand on the top of the girl's head.

"But she says she's a squirrel," I said. "What about imaginative play?"

The girl scowled at me. "You're stupid," she said. Marvin narrowed his eyes and said, "That's enough, young lady. Yancy may be many things, but she is not exactly stupid."

"Marvin, were you this strict with your own kids?" I asked.

"I'm pretty strict," said Marvin, beginning to smile.

The kid let go of Marvin, got down on her hands and knees, and crawled underneath the sandwich board. She peered around the edge to study the lettering. After a moment of mouthing sounds to herself, she said, "This … is … the … end." Then she crawled back out, dusted herself off, and reclamped her arm around Marvin's leg.

"You can read?" I asked her.

"I told you I'm in kindergarten," she said, and shoved her hand into her mouth.

"If you can read, you can certainly tell us your name, who your mommy is, and how you got here," said Marvin. He looked at me again, still smiling. "You can't let them take advantage of you. Trust me," he said.

The girl took her hand out of her mouth. "Mom dropped me off for Activity Summer," she said.

"Now we're talking," said Marvin, "So what's Activity Summer?"

"Activity Summer," said the kid.

"We don't know what that is," said Marvin, but he was in high spirits. "Jesus, you know what I think of this? I think this stinks. Did you just run off, is this what happened?"

"Activity Summer is where you play with the other kids. You have to do that, even if they're fat kids," the girl said.

"Be nice," said Marvin.

"Even if they're fat kids or not fat, but they wear huge jackets and they look just like marshmallows. Boy, I really hate that a lot."

"I used to hate that too," I said. I shrugged at Marvin's sharp glance.

"Yeah, but you have to play with them, Mommy said," continued the girl. "Like if you want to go on the merry-go-round, and they spin you too fast, or they won't spin you unless it's their turn or their dads are bossy. We don't like bossy dads. But you still have to play with them."

"This is during Activity Summer?" I asked.

"Okay," she sighed, "let's say we're on the teeter-totter, and I'm at the top, and I say 'Farmer Farmer, let me down,' and you say 'what will you give me Charlie Brown,' and I say 'One thousand pounds of food,' okay? What would you do?"

"I'd let you down," I said.

"Yeah, but some kids won't let you down. You have to give them like fifty mansions or something, and I really hate them. But you still have to play with them."

"But there aren't any other kids here. You're the only kid," said Marvin. He drummed his fingers on his jeans, and craned his neck to look around the park.

"I know. Mom said to wait for them and then Activity Summer would start. She said the best kids at Activity Summer make up their own activities. So I collected all the acorns in the park or something and I put them in a little nest. I did it all by myself. So you want me to show you it, Marvin?"

"I guess we'd better go see it," said Marvin.

"It's by the ocean," said the kid.

"It's actually called a lake," I said.

"How do you know?" asked the kid, "Have you been to a better ocean or something?" My insides sped up, lurching against something.

"I've seen pictures of it," I said. "The ocean, it'll sweep you up if you're not careful, you can't even imagine. This is a lake."

"No way," said the kid. "Lakes are way smaller. Way way smaller. A whole ton smaller. Mom said that's an ocean, like with sunked ships in it, I guess."

"Your mom told you that?" said Marvin. He shook his head. "See, that's how Shoshona was too. Anything they wanted, she told them. She told them they'd lose all their teeth, one by one, for Pete's sake, and then we'd change their names to Gummy One and Gummy Two, and they'd only be able to suck on melted cheese sandwiches for nutrition."

"Oh, yeah right," said the kid, adoring him. She hit her forehead against his knee a couple of times.

"That's what I'm saying," agreed Marvin. "It could never happen. Life with the three of them, it was like a year round Macy's parade, it was like existing in the belly of a downright unicorn."

"So stupid, or what," said the little girl. With vigor, she rubbed her nose back and forth against Marvin's calf.

"That's what I'm saying," said Marvin again. He carefully tilted the girl's head back, and detached his leg from her grip. He took her hand. Then he pulled down the orange and pink shade of the Sno-Cone cart window, and turned towards Sherman Lake. I strayed behind the two of them as we walked down towards the shore.

"Who's that?" I heard the girl ask, pointing back towards me.

"That? Well, that's Yancy," said Marvin.

"Is she a mommy?"

"Maybe someday."

"Are you in love with her?"

"It's really not what you think," said Marvin, and laughed a short note.

I laughed too, but I'll admit, seeing Marvin nurture this kid without even wanting to do it, I had been thinking how I could fasten him to my life in just that same way. Why did we act as though we were has-beens at the age of five years out of high school? There was still time to chuck it all out, start again, and no one would be the wiser.

I'll admit, I'd almost decided on Marvin Staples as my lethargic prince. He could take me to the ocean. But as I picked my way down the steep hill behind the two of them, my stomach turned bad. Someone, some adult, had taken this small girl by her sea-foam mitten, led her to the park, pointed to puny scum stagnant Sherman Lake and said:

This is it, kid.

This is all you need to know. The ocean? That crashing, life-stopping, deafening body? Forget it. Unimportant. The world consists of this lake. I watched Prince Marvin and the stubborn kid, and with finality I stopped strategizing for myself.

When we were most of the way down the hill, the girl let go of Marvin's hand to bend over a bare root nob jutting out of the frozen ground. It protected a cluster of acorns, half-submerged in a shallow hole.

"I made up this activity," she said. "Can I have a Sno-Cone now?"

"You can have some of mine," I offered. I still held the melting remnants.

"No," said Marvin, giving me that same sharp look. He was in his element, the look said, whether he liked it or not. As for me, I had no element. Marvin squatted down next to the kid. He said, "No Sno-Cone until you've had something along the lines of a mayonnaise-cheese sandwich, or a hot dog, or a bowl of Cheerios."

"Oh," I said. He and I looked at each other. The girl's face pinched up and she let out a long and wavering cry, a cry like a lamb on a bad day, on a steep hill, with the wind rushing angrily for us all the while.

"Oh, shit," said Marvin. He put one hand to his temple. "Don't cry," he said. "Please don't cry. It's not so bad."

"Boy, I hate Activity Summer," the girl hiccupped.

"We'll take you home now," said Marvin.

"We will?" I asked him.

"I want to take my acorns home with me," said the kid.

"Take them, by all means," said Marvin. The girl wiped her leaking nose with one mitten, and used the other to pull a tattered business envelope out of the sea-foam green fur pocket of her parka. There is no animal in nature with fur that color. The envelope was torn open roughly at one end, and she got to her knees and began to stuff acorns into it.

"Marvin," I said.

"I know," he said.

"Can I see that?" I asked the kid. "Just for a minute, can I look at that?"

She looked at Marvin.

"Yancy just wants to see the envelope," said Marvin. Warily, the kid handed it over.

The address on the envelope said *Agatha Hicks, 7373 American Camp Road.* The return address had been torn off. Other than the acorns, the envelope was empty.

"Is Agatha Hicks your mom's name?" I asked the girl.

"Agatha Hicks is my mom and me, and my grandma is Agatha Weems, and my aunt is Auntie Linda," she said. Marvin took the envelope from me.

"You're Agatha?" he asked the girl.

"Yes," she said. "Please can I have my acorns back now?" Marvin handed the envelope back to Agatha.

"Do you have a car, Yancy?" he asked me.

"Just my bike," I said.

"I have a car," he said, "but I have to run the Sno-Cone cart."

"Marvin, I don't know how to drive a car," I said.

"I know how to drive a car," he said. Desperation crept into the edge of his voice. "But running the Sno-Cone cart is something that's important to me. Look, Yancy, I've already been through this. I don't want to get in too deep."

He looked at Agatha, who was already beginning to walk up the hill. She walked sideways, streaking back and forth across the grade, the fine sea-foam fur of her hood haloing her red face. Marvin's face was all lonely capability and reluctance, and I could see that he was afraid. I could see it plainly, but as I said, I had stopped strategizing for myself.

"Marvin," I said.

He looked at me. "It just hurts like a broken rib," he said. "When Shoshona got pregnant, I was eighteen. I started working full time as a phone solicitor. I mean, she wanted a crib, a stroller, the works. It was like I never existed."

"Marvin," I said, "You have to drive us to American Camp Road."

"But," he said.

"Marvin," I said, "Come with me."

Marvin said, "Alright." He turned away up the hill.

Agatha mouthed words to herself, and as we caught up to her, she asked Marvin, "Why does your sign say 'This is the end'? Is it supposed to be scary or something?"

"It was supposed to say 'This is the end of winter,' for the purpose of advertising. But I ran out of space," explained Marvin.

"There aren't any kids around to eat your Sno-Cones, anyway," said Agatha.

"Nope, no kids," agreed Marvin, "no parents. None at all."

"None," said Agatha. They shook their heads. Agatha took Marvin's hand again, and marched him up the hill. The whole long way up, I could hear her murmuring, "Activity Summer, one thousand pounds of food, Activity Summer, this is the end, this is the end, this is the end."

Marvin locked up the Hawaii-Sno-Cone cart, and I tossed my soaked paper cone into a trash can, feeling my fingers sticky and numb, feeling the illogic of a Sno-Cone in March, and now I was here, doing this. At the edge of Ulysses Park, in the lot of the high school, I wedged my bike into the open trunk of Marvin's car, a bruised blue sedan. The inside was crumb ridden, and there was a lunch-box like car seat in the back. Agatha looked at it. "I'm too big for a car seat. I'm like sixty pounds heavy or something," she said.

"Trust me, Agatha. It's way more fun to be a baby," Marvin said. She climbed into the car seat, and Marvin buckled her in. "Goodbye, Activity Summer," she said quietly as we drove away, "See you next time."

"What do you think about Activity Summer?" I asked Marvin. "Forget activities, right? It's not even summer. It's March. Early March,"

"Tell me about it," Marvin said, "I'm thinking I should just close down the Sno-Cone cart. I'm losing money. This whole thing was a bad idea. What do you think?"

"I think you should take this whole thing a little more seriously," I said. "I think you've got to take some responsibility here."

"Look, we have to give Little Agatha back to Big Agatha, and that's what we're doing, right?" Marvin gripped the steering wheel and gulped once, looking at me out of the corner of his eye.

"But what if Big Agatha is a complete deadbeat?"

"What's 'deadbeat'?" asked Agatha.

"See?" asked Marvin, and his voice shook. "This is what I'm saying. She's a six-year-old. She's not deaf. If you could take a hint at all, instead of being like every other non-subtle, indiscreet woman on the planet earth, you could pick up on a hint and not talk about this issue in front of L-I-T-T-L-E A-G-A-T-"

"I get it," I said. In the back seat, Agatha was quiet.

"I'm sorry," said Marvin. "Not every woman on the planet is indiscreet. That wasn't fair."

"Don't worry about it," I said. "Anyway, you're right. I don't know anything about kids. I just try to be nice to them, and they can smell my inexperience like a dog smells fear. Agatha trusts you."

"When Shoshona got pregnant, people from high school said I was a broken man," said Marvin. He had stopped looking at me out of the corner of his eye and was staring hard at the road.

"I had such a crush on you in high school, I used to call you and hang up," I said.

"You did that?"

"Yes. I voted for you for homecoming king every year. You don't even remember that I existed."

"Yancy, sure I remember you."

"No, you don't. That's okay."

"I do, I do."

"I don't believe you. What do you remember?" I asked him, but we sat in silence until the sign for American Camp Road appeared on our left. We turned onto a gravel street, winding along a trash filled gully. Two cats picked along the gully, mean and lonely. In the back seat, Agatha had fallen asleep with her head back and her mouth open. She clutched her envelope. She sweated in her hood in the warm car. Marvin spoke.

"I didn't think you were the most attractive girl at our school, or even the second or third most attractive," he said.

"Who was?"

"Julia Cann, with that nest of hair, Tamara Bodkin with her gap teeth, and Stevo McCartney."

"Not a girl."

"But no one had arms like that guy, and I don't know if you remember this, but he used to ride his skateboard with rain boots on, and that moved me. Anyway, what about you?"

"What about me?"

"What have you been doing since high school?"

I thought for a moment. "I'm not going to lie to you," I said to Marvin. "I have had no novel published."

"You need to try harder," said Marvin. "Here we are: 7373." He pulled the car to a stop.

The houses along American Camp Road were fussy and small, one after another, each in the center of a sickly yellow lawn. When I looked at number 7373, I thought we must have made a mistake. The insubstantial pea green house looked empty and erupted. Full Garbage bags spilled down the cement stoop, bursting open. Empty cardboard boxes and Styrofoam packing peanuts littered the yard. The front door, wide open, banged against the house. The March wind blew dusty and bitter. It hadn't rained yet, though the dark sky hung heavy and close. A sign leaning against the steps said, "FREE STUFF: TAKE ANYTHING PLEASE."

"Wake up, Agatha," I reached back and tugged at one of her shoes. She jolted in her sleep, letting go of her acorn envelope, which fell to the floor of the car, and spilled its contents quietly as rain. She did not wake up.

"Might as well let her sleep," said Marvin, staring at the mess outside.

"Should we check it out?" I asked. He shook himself, and we got out of the car. We did not bother to knock first, and inside, the house smelled like air had only recently entered it at all. In the living room, there was a fireplace filled with broken glass, melted plastic, and one red high-heeled shoe. A glass coffee table had been upturned, and a plastic bowl lay near it, with Mickey Mouse's face encrusted in dried milk and one Cheerio. Someone had been sick on the carpet.

"Hello?" Marvin called. The smell of decay became overwhelming.

We saw the body at the same time. Splayed in the corner, barely visible in the hollow, dusk-lit, rotting room was a dog, dead, its legs stretched at odd angles. Its head was half off, the skull dashed open, and bits of red brains wormed out onto the carpet.

Not one person in my life has ever said to me, "The thing about kidnapping is how much sense it might make." March third, late afternoon, 7373 American Camp Road, for the first time I wished someone had.

Marvin and I stood side by side in the living room for a long time, neither of us using the time wisely for the purpose of discussing like two adults the evidence we were gathering. We stared at the mess, at the sick, at the dead dog with opaque eyes fast drying out. It was two minutes or more before we heard the sound, a sudden sound from the back of the house, and we turned quickly towards it. From the dark kitchen at the back, we heard a thin, scraping, scrabbling sound, and we both saw the shadow fall across the open door.

"Someone's in there," said Marvin. We left the house quickly, not touching.

We did not need to say much in the seconds it took us to get to the car. I could not tell him what was the right thing to do. Columbia Pinnacle or no Columbia Pinnacle, I did not know what was the right thing to do. I only knew, exact as one hot slap in the face, what we would do next.

"You'll take her," I said to Marvin, and he nodded once.

Inside the sedan, Agatha still dozed, her head lolling against the seat back. I lifted my bicycle out of the trunk of the car.

In spite of my desire to be the new me, I still half waited for Marvin to ask me to go with them, just so I could shake my head no, as far as that went. Just so I could remind him that Agatha didn't like me, and anyway, he and I barely knew each other, and anyway, just that split second, I had decided to try harder. I had decided my stories would have more shooting off of guns than ever before, except for those certain stories that began and ended quietly, that were written fervent and feminine as snow.

But he didn't ask. Instead that look came onto his face again, that close resolute look, precisely focused, impossible, at this last moment, to mimic. He knew, better than anyone else, what he could accomplish. He said, as he opened the driver's side door, "It wasn't fair, what I said earlier about women. And also, it's not that I don't take this seriously. I do. I believe in what we're doing."

"Where will you go?" I asked.

"California," said Marvin without hesitation, "the coast." I was an accomplice; an aider; an abetter. I was a co-conspirator. When he said it, my stomach eased up for what felt like the first time since Ulysses High.

He got into the car without looking at me again. As he turned the key in the ignition, Agatha opened her eyes, and sat up straight. "We're home!" she said happily, taking off her mittens to touch the window with her index finger. Marvin said something to her that I could not hear, but she smiled and waved to me, and then stuck her finger contemplatively in her nose. He started the engine, and drove away.

I swung onto my bike. I did not look back at 7373 American Camp Road. I pedaled along the gully, and turned right, back towards Ulysses Park, towards the lake, towards the community pool where, each summer, during day camp, a young person, always a young person drowns.

The Sno-Cone cart, when I rode past it was locked up and empty, the pink and orange striped shade drawn shut with finality. Only the sandwich board had been forgotten, and it falsely advertised the daily special: "Rootbeer Sno-Cone, Black Cherry syrup. THIS IS THE END…" A dusty orange cat, large and fibrous looking, like a dry husk of a kitten, skulked near the board. It was a cold day. It was a cold, cold day. I stooped forward from my bicycle and reached out to the tomcat. In a flash, he thrust his claws forward, hissing, and tore open my hand. I wrenched back, and the cat streaked away, disappearing into the park.

My hand throbbed and swelled with cat scratch poison. I let my bike fall to its side at the top of the hill, and I retraced my steps down to Sherman Lake. I had to climb over a chain link fence to get to the water. I plunged my arm in up to the elbow, and watched fine threads of blood climb to the surface. It was only after my submerged hand was numb from the cold, floating still, bright, and drowned, that I tilted my head upwards and noticed the sign above me, attached to the fence. "Danger. Water May Burn or Sting Flesh. Do Not Drink, Do Not Swim. Wash Thoroughly If Accidental Contact Occurs."

Marvin Staples was missing, Agatha Hicks was missing, Agatha Hicks was missing too. The next day, I left the town where I had grown up a day at a time, always with sour, nervous breath, and I made for the shining sea.

THE STARS AND
STRIPES FOREVER

During the summer, Hogan Robedeaux, who was in my daughter Marnie's grade at school, was burned almost to death, but not quite. He came back to life, but would always, from head to toe, look like what the kids at school thought an alien would look like. He was made of wax suddenly. Only a round patch on his face had been spared. He was ten years old, and had previously been the least mean of all his mean brothers and sisters, but after his accident most things just slipped into the reverse of what they'd been before. Awed into pale ghostly things, his siblings stopped spitting their gum into people's hair, and stopped holding the nerds down to fart on their heads, and stopped ambushing Alfie, the tiny first grade epileptic, to make him fall over and wet his pants. After Hogans's accident, his brothers and sisters stalked the playground with their mouths and eyes dry, like they were afraid to be ripped at any moment out of the world. At the same time, Hogan grew large, larger, vivid and angry like a scar, like a lesion in our lives. People get tired of that kind of thing no matter what. Before I knew about the trouble with Hogan and my daughter Marnie, I sometimes wanted to take tender hold of the edge of that small soft circle leftover on his face. I wanted to peel Hogan, and underneath find him again, white and slimy and fuzzy, like a new stem. But the thing is, he already had no skin anymore, and no one was allowed to touch him because it hurt him like hell all over again. It could kill him, that kind of pain. That was rule number one.

―――

Hogan Robedeaux was the only one of his family to not get out of the car before the fire started, and his parents, realizing he would never do anything so bracing and rough as ride his BMX bike again, and being wealthy, frankly the wealthiest, and belonging to the country club, and smelling like cherry lip gloss, these kind of people, they donated Hogan's BMX to the Bikes for Tykes program at the Center. All this about Hogan and his accident and the perfect round circle on his face I found out later, after I had already brought the BMX home for Marnie. She could already do a few tricks on it by the time I knew it was the ex-bicycle of a burned boy, whose fingers and toes were melted together the way Marnie's had been webbed since birth, and in fact the Robedeaux children used to make fun of her about it until their great silent change.

But like I said, by that time, Marnie could do a few tricks on the BMX, which Ernie taught her to do, which they didn't include me in, or even seem to remember I was the one who'd found her the bike in the first place. Ernie taught Marnie to jump on and off the curb with that tiny bike, and I watched them out the window in the last few evenings of the summer. The Robedeauxs lived all the way across town, in a house with a green lawn like the fur of a stuffed animal, and I didn't know exactly where their car had exploded or anything like that. Our neighborhood was low and quiet and full of bikes and broken screen doors and empty crates and box springs on porches like the owners didn't actually care about how those porches looked, which I understood.

I watched Marnie from the window and her body was already too big for that tiny bike. Her glasses were too small for her huge head. It wasn't that my Marnie was fat. She'd just been born like Paul Bunyan, in a legendary and hulking way. I could love it easily because before she was right here with us, she'd grown that way inside my body somehow. I made her that way. Well, Ernie and me together. I watched Ernie coach Marnie. She hefted up on the BMX and lifted it into the air. They were setting up something secret, and later, when they came into dinner, Marnie ate as much stew as I could keep up with putting in front of her. She ate like a construction worker, like a man twice Ernie's size, and we were proud of her, Ernie and I. It was all we had in common.

When Marnie was born, Ernie sat forward and watched like he had just now figured out what all those months of me getting so big had been for, which made me think, was my husband even a grown man? Then, on the other hand, Marnie was a miracle, and I can hardly believe I was there for it. The doctors said there was something wrong with her, and I guess they meant the tissue paper webbing between her fingers and toes, or the fact that she was fifteen pounds, three ounces, and could hold her head up and look all around. They told me something was wrong with her, but I didn't believe it. From the beginning, Marnie grew like there was nothing else she wanted to do with her time on the planet but get gigantic. She came out big and furry as a baby bear.

For years, Ernie chopped wood to heat the house. Long before what our marriage came to amount to, I stood at that window and watched his back and the muscles in it networking upwards, and his legs straddled out, and his feet planted surely apart. I watched him at it for years in sickness and health.

The November when Marnie was six years old, I came home one day from the Center to find Ernie standing at the window with his back to me, staring out into the backyard. When he turned from the window, he had nothing to say to me. He traveled a distance of blind miles to the sofa and just kind of sprawled there, and it was about the first time I noticed his body was shrinking. He didn't have any look on his face but confusion and defeat.

I went to the window and looked out. Marnie was back there. With each swing of the axe her arms strove against her T-shirt. At that time, Marnie already weighed one hundred and thirty pounds, and was five feet, two inches tall, with a red face, wide and glad. Her hair was growing ropey and yellow, her eyes were failing already, her teeth were strong and square. Marnie was warm as a humming motor all the time. I watched my daughter split wood, and it was the axe melting hot through each log that did it, it was that fast.

From the sofa, Ernie said dully, "She wanted to try. At first I thought, what the hell, it'll be cute, right? So I held the axe with her."

Outside everything was blurry and shiny. Everything was wet so that you sank straight into the ground. Marnie stood straight there steaming. Her vigorous breaths told me she would live forever.

"She didn't need me," said Ernie.

"She could hurt herself," I said. But I made no move to stop her. She would live forever, I thought. There is nothing about her I would change.

"I couldn't keep up," Ernie said, and continued to lie there like something broke.

Marnie chopped all the wood, which became the way things were.

Ernie switched the TV on. It was company, the TV. It was like having real people around. Separately, we were proud of Marnie, and looked at her together without breathing.

Hogan Robedeaux had always been a real hotshot. Hanging by his knees from the monkey bars, he was not afraid to throw himself out into the air and kick up sawdust as he twisted to land solid on his feet. With his BMX bike, he skidded down the railing on the front steps of the school. During prison ball, Hogan's classmates covered him, pinning him up against the fence in a teeming crush of bodies because he was the most valuable player, and they would not, under any circumstances, let him go to prison. In the matter of Boys Chase Girls, Hogan caught a girl, Becky Shell, the pinkest and purplest girl in school, and he knew exactly what he wanted to do with her. He grabbed both of her hands and pulled her with him through to the other side of the sprinkler, and there, they stuck their tongues in each other's mouths. That was when Hogan was nine years old, and during the summer he turned ten, Marnie and Becky Shell went to horseback riding camp together.

"Everybody likes you, Becky Shell," said Marnie on the bus. "You're cute."

"What do you mean?" asked Becky Shell, flushing.

"You look like a little monkey." Marnie was solemn. Becky Shell frowned and snickered. They held hands all the way to camp. They held hands all they way back, and when I met their bus, Becky Shell cried and wouldn't let go of Marnie. Marnie gently detached herself and waved goodbye as the bus pulled away. On the way home, I noticed she wore a bracelet, made of plastic twine, hot pink. Marnie turned it around and around her wrist. At home Ernie was waiting with the new bike I'd brought home from the Center the day before. "Becky Shell says I'm the strongest kid in school," said Marnie. She leaned her head back on the seat, and her face was fierce and wistful. "That girl," she said. "That Becky Shell."

That first day of school after the accident, Hogan Robedeaux sat in the front of the room, and turned around to meet everyone's staring. The teacher, blinking back tears, read a note from the principal, about the tragedy etc, about sympathy etc, about how he was just the same on the inside etc, and most of all, in capital letters in fact, that if anyone so much as touched Hogan Robedeaux they would be expelled from school. Expelled, did the class understand her? Which they did, and they swore they would leave him standing alone during prison ball, circling around him so widely that he could not even feel the wind from their rushing bodies. They swore that if they were on the opposing team, they would not throw the ball at Hogan to try to get him into prison. They would never throw the ball at him, or near him again, but would in fact calculate the farthest point away from Hogan Robedeaux and only throw the ball there. Somehow they swore that if he ever happened to get hold of the ball, they would all stand with bated breath hearing in their imaginations the perplexing humor of grown ups saying, "Please Don't Break That Priceless Ming Vase," and let Hogan take aim and hit them squarely with the ball. Helpless as bowling pins, they would go to prison, and they wouldn't even care.

In her seat by the window Becky Shell also swore never to touch Hogan Robedeaux again, and she bit her lip where she used to have bite marks from him, and she scratched her upturned monkey nose with her eraser which was shaped like a unicorn, which smelled like peaches, but not real peaches. She squirmed in her purple sun suit, and she stared at Marnie, who sat with her large jaw clenched and her heavy webbed fingers sweating on the desk, squinting through her glasses across the room at Hogan, even as every other kid in the class earnestly studied every other part of the classroom besides the Hogan part. Hogan Robedeaux took it all in. He saw the way Becky Shell looked at Marnie, and the way Marnie looked at him like her heart might not go on beating much longer from pity. He saw he was sentenced to phantomness. He followed all those gazes, and after that it was war.

Marnie approached Hogan as he walked out of school, flanked by his brothers and sisters. She held out her hands. "Mine have been webbed since I was born," she said, "My feet, too."

"That's because you're a freak," he said. "You're an ogre, you're a troll, you're the hulk, you're a duck girl, you're a monster, you're a geek, a freak. Haven't you ever looked at yourself?"

Marnie was used to the way the other kids saw her, and mostly they left her alone because they had seen the way she spun the merry-go-round so fast it began to buzz and lift off the ground, and they had seen her throw the prison ball so far past the prison it disappeared into the recess sky, and no one ever found that prison ball again. The exceptions to this were the Robedeaux children, who used to sing safe from the top of the jungle gym, "*Oh, be kind to your web footed friend, for a duck may be somebody's mother...*" and so on, to the tune of *The Stars and Stripes Forever*.

Now Hogan tried to strike up a chorus of it, raising his melted hands to conduct. But his brothers and sisters shifted around in their shoes, and looked at anything, anything, besides Marnie and Hogan, and they coughed and one of them farted nervously, and then they shuffled on out of there. They weren't likely to be in the mood ever again. As Hogan followed his family, all tuckered out and lonesome, Marnie blinked. That's all she did. It wasn't so mean, what those siblings had put her through. It wasn't half as bad as the bald fear she got from everyone else, and now it was over.

Hogan's campaign of war was a scorched earth policy, and he operated with complete impunity. Every morning, he waited in the park along the school, and when Marnie passed him, he ripped off her backpack, and stole her homework for the day. Rather than fight back, Marnie immediately froze when Hogan approached her, arms held away from her body for easy backpack ripping. She was terrified of touching Hogan, who yelled into her face, "Stay away from Becky Shell, Marnie. Leave Becky Shell alone." He tore her homework to confetti, and ran into school as the last bell rang. Marnie was weeping and late. Grown ups would have told her to tell the teacher. Marnie didn't tell. Hogan collected all the hamster shit from Hercules, the classroom hamster, and filled Marnie's desk with it. Marnie stayed in at recess and cleaned it up quietly with paper towels from the girls' bathroom. She washed her hands. She didn't tell anyone. Hogan stuck his fried little foot out to trip Marnie when she lumbered past him, and when she fell headlong to the floor, he would hiss over her, "Do you want to get expelled, Marnie? Touch me. Come on, Marnie. I dare you. I dare you." Marnie picked herself up, and walked gingerly away, heaving and red, but not about to touch Hogan at all. Not even close.

Becky Shell came over to play most days. When I picked the girls up from school, I saw Hogan watching them together. I felt a pain in the place I reserved for admitting to myself that Marnie was a human being, and that human beings eventually grew up, moved away, and died. It was a pain in the order of things, and Hogan's scarred body cracked that order. I looked around for his mother or father, but they were elsewhere, at that moment exploring expensive strategies for setting their family back in place, and they couldn't touch their son. If they loved him, they could barely touch him. All I could see were the other Robedeaux children, lined up like soldiers, and even from where I stood I didn't expect them to have that cherry lip gloss smell anymore. And I didn't expect anyone to yearn to take hold of that soft circle on Hogan's head except me.

We were on speaking terms that day, so I told Ernie I thought it was wonderful Marnie finally had a friend.

"You should never have sent her to horseback riding camp," he said.

"How can you disapprove of Becky Shell?" I asked him. "She's got to be the sweetest little monkey ever created."

"You should never have sent her to that camp. She's become oversexed."

"Don't be disgusting. She's a kid. Kids form attachments. She never takes that bracelet off. I think she's going to let it decompose on her wrist."

"A monkey may love a bear, but where will they find a home together?"

We were firing past each other, the way you might shoot at a wall behind someone's head, in order to show them what you're made of. I saw Ernie caving in, not giving way, but moving over, shrinking to make room for illness and anger, and it's not that we were poor, it's that my husband was lazy. He was lazy, he really was. And he wanted someone to pay.

In the next room, the girls ate plates of ginger cookies and laughed at each other through the crumbs. Becky Shell said, "Why don't you kick his butt, Marnie? Who even cares about his stupid burned butt? Not me."

"What's that?" I called, interrupting Ernie, "Who's butt?"

"Come on, I'll show you how to do tricks on my BMX," said Marnie, ignoring me. Their chairs scraped back. Ernie went after them. "I'll show you," I heard him say as they went out into the yard together, "I'll show you girls what to do." He left the TV talking to itself. The thing about Ernie was that he liked to have a secret plan with someone all the time. When we met, he liked to have a secret plan with me. Now it was Marnie. I watched them out the window.

Marnie ignored Hogan when he chased her after school and threw eggs at her. She cleaned up in the bathroom before I saw a thing. When he cut up magazines into eloquent death threats, Marnie cut them up all over again into secret notes for Becky Shell. When he wrote "OGRE" across her desk, breaking the tips of three pencils in the process, Marnie scrubbed it off, using up three pink erasers and breaking one pencil in half with the pressure. Hogan taunted her daily, "You can't do crap, Marnie," he said, "Unless you want to get expelled. I dare you, Marnie, I dare you to touch me." But Marnie never did. At night sometimes, she snuffled and cried with frustration over her homework, and she chopped wood like the sun was about to go out.

It was three o'clock, Wednesday afternoon. Marnie and Becky would be home soon, and Ernie and I waited, not talking, in front of the TV news. A story came on about a mother grizzly bear who, two days before, had mauled a hiker in Alaska. The hiker was in critical condition, and in checking into his records, the hospital found out he was a divorced father of three who had not paid any child support in three years. The newscasters were delighted, and across the screen flashed the words, "Angry Mama Mauls Deadbeat Dad."

"I could do that to someone. I'm like that mama bear," Ernie said. The screen showed a picture of the deadbeat dad. Half his face was gone.

"Oh, you are not. The one who's like that is Marnie."

"You are completely missing my goddamn point. Marnie is not a mother. She's a child."

"You're not a mother, either, Ernie."

"I'm a parent. Okay? I could kill any man who messed with my kid. Kill him quick as quick." Ernie was already raising his voice.

"Kill him?" I asked.

"Dead. No problem. Violently dead."

"That's terrible," I said. "You're being stupid. There are other ways to solve problems."

"You're being stupid is who's being stupid. Thank God I'm around."

"Thank who, exactly? Who's thanking God, here?"

"Now you're not making sense," and so on, and so forth. We were sweating at it, which was a change from how cold we could be, but we were still angry, and not in a way that brought us closer, when we heard Marnie's sneakers pound up the porch. We heard the screen door slam, and then our gargantuan daughter, panting with those impressive lungs of hers, stood there in front us. She looked from one to the other of us quite calmly. She said, "I'm sorry, I really am. But I'm going to have to get expelled from school."

That's when Marnie told us the entire one sided war story, up to today, when she told us it was not going to be one sided anymore. She told us how Hogan had followed her and Becky Shell after school, as they began to walk home together through the park. Hogan stayed behind them, and pelted them with pine cones for a good quarter mile. "It's okay, Becky. Just ignore him," said Marnie.

"We can't touch him," said Becky.

"I know," said Marnie. She handed Becky her 3-ring binder to hold up as a shield. But then Hogan caught up with them. Marnie thought he might attack her, but she didn't expect him to attack Becky Shell, which is what he did. He tore her sunsuit. Becky stood like a stone, and wouldn't look at him. She didn't say a thing. She looked at Marnie. Marnie screamed and she was huge, bigger than any of the teachers or anyone, she screamed but they were deep in the park, and no one came. Hogan, bigger than Becky, but not by much, tore Becky's sun suit off her body, until she stood in her undershirt and underpants, knees touching. Then he hauled her over his shoulder, took her to the nearest tree, lifted her up, and hung Becky Shell there, by her unicorn underpants, suspended only five feet off the ground but it seemed like more. It caused Hogan a lot of physical pain to do that, but he went ahead and did it anyway. "You can't do anything to me," he said to them. "If you touch me, I might die." Then he went home.

Becky hung there, staring at Marnie. Marnie tried to help her down, but Becky twisted and kicked her. "Don't touch me," she shrieked, "Don't you touch me, Marnie."

With a long tearing sound, her underpants came apart, and she fell to the ground. She collected her shredded clothes around her, and started running back across the park. Marnie followed her. "We couldn't touch him," she pleaded.

"Don't touch me," Becky Shell repeated. She ran as fast as she could for home. And then there was Marnie, in front of Ernie and me, all alone, dry eyed and resolved. "I'm sorry," she said. "I have to get revenge."

I stood aghast while Ernie nodded and thought it over. After a moment, he said, "I'll tell you exactly what you have to do." But then he looked at me, and I saw him adding something up. He put his arm on Marnie's muscle bound back. "Come on," he whispered to her, and led her out into the garage, which I felt at that point like, I'm part of this team too. But they didn't seem to notice, and that was always how it was. I went over to the TV and turned it off. But the newspaper on the coffee table said the same thing: "Angry Mama Mauls Deadbeat Dad."

The next morning, I tried to put Marnie's lunchbox into her backpack for her, but she grabbed it out of my hand.

"I'm riding my BMX to school today," she told me, and slammed out the door. Ernie walked into the kitchen, scratching, as I was about to leave for the Center. "Marnie's gone already? Damn, that boy's going to be sorry," he said and when he laughed, I wasn't sure if Ernie was more or less lazy than I'd previously thought, but I was sure of something more ugly and terrible than any secret I'd imagined.

"What's she going to do?" I asked him slowly.

"We thought up a way she could do it without touching the little bastard," he said.

"Tell me, Ernie," I said, but he just shook his head, proud.

"Jesus," he said. "Sometimes I think of her swallowing up the whole ocean, and then just eating up all the fish," I was out the door before I heard if that led to anything else.

Driving, I caught up with Marnie riding her bike straight as an arrow over all the cracks in the sidewalk. She was almost to the park. I pulled up along side her, and out the window, I said, as friendly as I could, "Marnie, why don't you get in, and I'll take you the rest of the way."

"What for?" she asked, keeping straight on.

"I thought I might go talk to the principal about what happened," I said, "Or to your teacher."

"No need. Me and dad figured it out," she said, but she swerved and glanced over at me.

"What's the plan, Marnie?" I asked, and she sighed and stopped her bike. She told me how Ernie had found an empty gas can in the garage, and rinsed it out, filled it with cold water, then screwed the lid on tight. Marnie unzipped her backpack and showed me the can, then held up a paper book of matches. She smiled with those square choppers of hers. "It's just a joke," she said, "But that boy's going to be sorry." She sounded exactly like Ernie. She began riding her bike again. All I could do was follow, calling her name like a bird.

At the border of the park, Hogan waited for her as usual. As soon as I saw him, I stopped the car and got out. "Stay right there, Hogan!" I called, but he paid no attention to me. He was looking at Marnie. It was the first time she'd ridden the BMX to school, and the sight of Marnie riding his old bicycle strongly towards him seemed to mesmerize Hogan, and shake his whole body.

"Marnie, I forbid you. I forbid you—" I began but she cut me off, pointing at Hogan.

"You're not going to steal my homework again. You're not going to trip me again. You're never going to touch Becky Shell ever again, Hogan Robedeaux, not ever again."

Hogan just kept staring at his BMX. The circle on his face had sweat on it, and fine hair. I stepped towards him, but he backed away. In war, both sides have their strategies. It was then that I saw that he was holding a silver pair of scissors.

Hogan Robedeaux ducked swiftly towards Marnie, and she didn't know what he wanted. He lunged with the scissors, nearly knocking Marnie over, and then he twisted around her body and darted cleanly out with the blades. Just like that, snip, snip, snip, he did what we'd never decided to do surgically, what we never thought to change about our Marnie. He cut through the webbing on her right hand, and by the time Marnie jerked herself backwards, falling off her bike, holding her hand up, throwing blood all around, three of her fingers were separate as souls.

Maybe I made noise, but for sure what I did was pick up the gas can from where it had fallen from Marnie's backpack. I scrambled for the matches. I looked at Marnie, waving her ruined hand around and thought of her as a perfect furry baby, her fingers and toes bound together, making her the new design for humans everywhere. Surely we would not remain the way we were. I unscrewed the cap without thinking another thing. I opened the gas can. Hogan backed away doubtfully, but I followed him step for step. I was the worst thing he could ever dream up, and I emptied the gas can over his head, soaking him completely. Water, that's all it was, but he hadn't realized it yet. When I lit the match, and threw it towards him, he closed his eyes. Descending into the nightmare of fire, he fell backwards to the ground.

Marnie stood stock solid still and watched me do what I did.

Could you kill a man if your kid was threatened, asked Ernie, implying that he could, he certainly could, but he didn't think I could do it, not me. But if what Ernie amounted to was a man who could stay home and wave goodbye to his child as he sent her off quick as quick with a can of gasoline in her backpack, if he was that kind of coward, then what was I? Could I kill a man, like a mama bear could? When I let go of it, the empty can of gasoline struck the ground hollow and toppled to its side.

One of Marnie's hands grasped the other, and blood squeezed out around her knuckles. It made red trails down her hands, and pooled in the creases of her elbows.

Hogan lay on the grass, gasping and gasping. He turned over and retched. Hogan's body was twisting, and his face was one big hole, except for the circle which magnified towards me, white and fleshy. Now was the time to peel.

Then Marnie shuttled herself down on the grass, wiping her bloody hands on her blue jeans. Her glasses fell off. Her yellow hair fell in ropes across her face. She touched Hogan Robedeaux. She grabbed firmly his hip bone, and the rounded part of his shoulder and she didn't say anything exactly, but she murmured a hushing sound. All the rules were broken.

Hogan Robedeaux lay still. His breathing slowed and his body relaxed from her touch, and he cried, at my feet, me still standing there useless, could I kill a man? At my feet, a ten year old boy, a real hotshot, a small humming motor, he cried and cried.

Marnie began to sing quietly as she held Hogan. Though the words didn't matter, she sang, "*Oh, be kind to your web footed friends, for a duck may be somebody's mother.*" She touched his damaged eyelids, she touched his collar bone, she touched his webbed hand, she touched the circle on his head, and I don't know where I got the idea that circle was perfect, because nothing is perfect. Not, especially not, this circle, which as I looked closer was more the shape of a red potato, and was most likely caused by a piece of flying shrapnel in the car accident, and anyway, even if it was perfect, it was meaningless.

"*And she lives in the swamp all alone, where it's cold and dark and damp,*" Marnie continued, coming to the last line of that song, which was so funny and abrupt, like suddenly falling off the edge of a wall, your arms wheeling comically in thin air. The end of the song was, to the tune of *The Stars and Stripes Forever*, "*Now you may think that this is the end. Well it is.*"

THE STORM BEACH

When I was a boy on the Island, before I could imagine any other place, each day came at me menacing and brilliant. The boat capsized, and if you stayed in the Sound for over twenty minutes, you were sure to die of the cold, people fell to the rocks, red tide rolled in and made the shellfish into poison traps, raccoons ate their babies season by season with some misguided instinct about protecting them. "Oh, those cannibals," Grandmother would shake her head, hissing at them like a mad cat to shoo them away from the porch. There were beautiful times, too.

Granddad took me in his freckled arms when I was three days old, and he sat me in Grandmother's largest wooden mixing bowl, and he balanced his way down the black rocks to the Storm Beach. Pissing on myself and howling, I didn't look at all like the hero he hoped I would become one day, but he baptized me in salt water, and one thing about the modern world is, you're not allowed to just do whatever you want to do with your dead anymore.

You're not allowed to heap up beech bark out on the Storm Beach, stick a sheaf of Winston Churchill's best speeches in your Granddad's breast pocket, and light the whole thing on fire. Not even if you'd always promised him you would. All he was trying to do, when he told me gravely to dedicate my life to sloth and avarice, was to show me that I could make up my own religion, my own method, my own blueprint reason. I took him at his word. I told my Grandmother I would do it. I definitely didn't expect her to do it. And it had to be done. It rang through me, the only thing that made a bit of sense because, as a rule, he'd been an animist.

When I heard Granddad was sick, I left the city straightaway to come back to the Island, traveling by train, then car, then hitching a ride in Virgil's aluminum speed boat out of Snug Harbor. Virgil left me at the head of our dock. I could tell he'd been wanting to say something to me the whole ride over, from the way he chewed away at nothing back by the motor, and didn't even ask me to help with the bow line. Sure enough, he called out above the wind, "Hope you don't expect me to pick you back up any time soon. You oughta stay put for a while. Your Grandmother needs you now." I raised my hand, but only to keep my watch-cap pulled down over my ears. Virgil wanted me to know that he went where he pleased. He wanted me to know he followed the shoals of herring. So what? Everyone did what they liked. When I'd wanted to leave the

Island, I left it. I cried too, sometimes. My Grandmother never told me it was wrong for a boy to do that. You hear about that sometimes, in other families.

Up the aerie path, the madrona bark slid underfoot like warm human skin, and at the cabin, I saw the freezer hooked up to the generator out back and I knew I was too late. With all the power it took to keep that thing cold, Grandmother knew I would feel guilty. And I did. I knew then that it was up to me to carry out Granddad's wishes.

Grandmother was in her garden, putting up chicken wire around her tomatoes to keep the deer away, but I could see her heart wasn't in it. Anyway, the deer, nibbling with their long still snouts, trampled the chicken wire, and they would have trampled my Grandmother, too, who, as I watched, dropped to her knees among the tomato plants and began to dig with her hands through the soil. Time was, the deer were afraid to come so close to us on the Island, but I could see those days were gone with my Granddad. I knew I was nowhere near the man he was. Now, the deer crept close, the foxes crept close, everything just closed in on us. The grey foxes, at the far end of the porch, put their noses in at the screens.

I stood on the steps Granddad had built out of twisted salt wood from the Storm Beach, and before I said anything, Grandmother turned her fine dark eyes towards the cabin and saw me. She dropped her arms to her sides and sat up on her knees, and then her face crumpled to tissue paper, and her high voice came like a child's protest, "Drat it all, Edmond. I've lost my wedding ring. Just now, when

I was chasing off the deer. They'll eat up all my kitchen if I can't stay vigilant. And then, I looked down, and my ring finger's bare for the first time in fifty years. Gone, just like that. And of all things, on the day he goes. What does Henry mean by it?" A keening cry, a blue heron call came up out of her and she settled to her side in the dirt.

"Grandmother," I said, and I went to her in the garden, hissing the deer away into the woods. We knelt in the patch of sandy earth, side by side beneath her tomatoes. When she quieted, we began to dig around in the sand for her hard gold ring. We found three cobwebbed snails, and a spotted clam shell the breadth of her eyelid.

"How did you get him in the freezer all by yourself?" I asked her.

"How did I get him in there? I just heaved him in, didn't I? I was a nurse at one time, you'll remember. I didn't always dash around serving that old man."

But I didn't remember. It's just and right that your grandparents should die when you're in your twenties, and I'd made it all the way to twenty-nine with the two of them none the worse for wear, holding fast to their impenetrable British citizenship, Granddad still supplying Grandmother with the kind of single-minded male attention that borders on abuse. Somehow, she took it. The final winter before I left the Island, a Douglas Fir crushed the cabin roof, and so we moved into the Wickiup until Spring. I'd stay out late each afternoon so they could do whatever it is they did. They were seventy-five and eighty, respectively, so I imagine their version of the sex act was not much reflected in mass media, but the Wickiup only had the one room so I had to face the fact that they wanted me out. I took long walks. Granddad was a real old perv, and Grandmother, well, all I can say is that he died on a dead-end Easter Sunday, and she sat beside me in the garden, and burrowed like a rabbit for her wedding ring. With her short legs stuck out in front of her, Grandmother looked like a small girl, except for her open old face, awash with what she had lost.

We couldn't find the ring, and the light was fading down the length of the Island, settling down into Puget Sound. I said, "Let's go inside, I'll make you some supper."

She stuck the point of her tongue between her front teeth. "I don't know why we never taught you to cook," she said. "We had the time, Lord knows. Yes, but we just relaxed instead. We set by the fireplace, we drank tea, let's see, oh yes, we laced our tea with gin. Oh, that's nice. Let's have some gin."

"Come inside, I'll make you a hot toddy." I took her arm, but she shook me off with harsh force.

"Edmond, now. We've got to do our duty. I'll make you a thermos of tea and whiskey. That's what you fancy anyway, isn't it? Gin is for old women, I think. Like me. Then, I'll look for my ring until it's too dark to see."

"I'll help you," I said.

"No," she said.

"I'll help you, Grandmother," I said, but she looked me level in the eye, her lashes long and dusty.

"Edmond, I won't sleep tonight with Henry in that freezer. He'd never stand for it. We never use that generator, Edmond. I don't think we've used it since before you were born. It's a frivolous expense." She went for the thermos.

The ATV was broken down, and I'd never learned to fix it, or drive it, or drive anything. Or even drive the boat, which I guess was what Virgil meant down at the dock. But I was good at some things, and I rolled the rusted green wheelbarrow up to the freezer, and I opened the freezer. Inside, Granddad stared up at me, not looking like he was alive or anything. Looking like he was dead. My Grandmother came out and set the thermos on the porch steps. She moved to her rosemary boxes by the kitchen window, and she clucked her tongue. "That ring. It would be unacceptable to Henry if I've lost it, if I've really lost it. Did you ever see the picture of him when we were married?" I had, and it looked like he was about twelve years old, with a hollowed shock about his eyes that would stay with him his whole life.

He hadn't been in the freezer long, only since that afternoon. Looking down at him with the sort of patience I never had while he was alive, I saw that Granddad wore clothing identical to mine. His woolen shirt was Blackwatch tartan. Mine was a plain red hunting color, but they were the same. My scarf was the same one knotted around his neck, too, an Aran knit I recognized because Grandmother had made us each one for that final Christmas, the one we spent together in the Wickiup. That whole

morning, he farted and scowled and stoked up the woodstove, while I tried to make it through my almanac of pa-
gan gods for no reason at all. We were irritable, we were
itchy, we felt like we had scales. At the end of that day,
after we'd suffered through the roast goose ordered from
Snug Harbor, our eyes disappeared into the swelling rust
of our cheeks, and we had to take to our bunks. We'd been
allergic to some wild harvested greens Grandmother had
forced on us for breakfast, and we fumed stricken on our
backs for the next three days, furious and scabby.

Granddad was a smaller man than me, a skinny spare
man who looked at larger men with disdain, as if their
girth was proof of their impotence. He was under six feet
tall and strong as a catapult. Grandmother outweighed
him all their lives together, and he was proud of that,
boasting of how her bare brown thighs spilled out from
her mannish woolen underwear. He was small and white
and freckled, and when I leaned into the freezer and gathered him in my arms, his ribcage lifted against his shirt.
He was cold, but he wasn't exactly heavy. It's just that his
reluctant limbs seemed at odds, and his limp weight was
particularly contrary, and he didn't help me a bit, being
once and for all actually dead. I managed to load him
into the green wheelbarrow, but there was no way to stop
it from being cartoonish. I only hoped Grandmother
wouldn't see, but she was still busy looking for her ring,
and she had moved to search through the woodpile by the
door. I couldn't carry the thermos, so I took a long drink
of it, and then left it steaming on the steps.

Granddad's arms fell free from the back of the wheelbarrow, and traced long trails behind him along the Aerie trail as I rolled him down towards the Storm Beach. His fingers rapped along tree roots polished to copper red with use. His body jostled back and forth, tipping dangerously over the sides of the barrow, while his stiffening legs bounced gently out in front. I strove to keep my footing. On the dappled water below us, the wind off the bay raised cat's paws, and when it calmed for a moment, I saw a seal raise its slick dark head out of the water, curious, without any moral compass.

When I reached the cape over the Storm Beach, I had to leave the wheelbarrow. There was no way to maneuver it down the rocks. I thought of slinging Granddad over my shoulder, but I couldn't do it when I tried. I got his torso up over my shoulder, but then his arms wouldn't stay put. They listed to one side, and dragged his carriage towards the ground, and then his legs jutted straight out like levers, and swung me off balance.

So I sat in the dusk on the cape, the wind drying out my eyes and lips, with Granddad's hoary head in my lap, his right arm splayed out beside him, twisted so that his flat grey palm covered the ground. He still had his smell, a smell that always irritated me. He smelt of his belief that eating popcorn made on the woodstove would save him. Well, it hadn't saved him. I knew his favorite thing was ice cream, and I knew he hadn't tasted it for years.

The lighthouse over on Nelson Bay sounded its evening tone. Below me on the Storm Beach, the tide rose up and dipped against the flat white-ringed boulder we used for roasting a lamb each August. Granddad's eyes began to attract mosquitoes, even though it seemed too cold for mosquitoes. I had to do something. So I got to my feet, and I hoisted Granddad by his armpits. His head lolled back and thudded against the ground, but I was past reminding myself that he couldn't feel a thing, and I dragged him down the rocks like that. He was wearing the canvas boat shoes he'd died in, and his feet bounced and twisted against the rocks, and his ankles were pretty well torn up by the time I got him down to the shore. I propped him up against that big flat stone.

I built the fire the way I had each August since boyhood, collecting beech bark by the armful, up and down the high tide line, carrying it to the roasting stone, heaping the pile high. I had forgotten my gloves—it was Spring for Christ's sake, it was Easter Sunday—but the salt rubbed my hands raw, and a green crab crawled from under a grey stone and pinched me until I bled. I flung it as far as I could out into the bay.

By the time the moon rose, I'd mounded the beech bark as high as my shoulder. I had stopped noticing the tide until I felt it lash at my shoes, and I turned and saw that Granddad's body lay half submerged in saltwater, his hands floating back and forth in the seaweed. Green crabs struggled along Granddad's shoulders and crept over his face, pulling at his Pendleton shirt, nibbling at the scratchy skin where he stopped shaving. Cursing, I plunged into the water, brandishing a club of driftwood, and I beat at my Granddad's body until all the crabs were gone. Then I dragged him over to the pile of beech bark, his heels plowing up the pebbles to make the sand fleas hop. He'd grown waterlogged. I pushed and pulled him. I dislocated both of his shoulders, I twisted his left knee out of its socket, but I got him up onto his funeral pyre. And I set it aflame.

The wind from Haro Straight pummeled past me, caught the flames, raged the flames through the beech bark, and when I first smelled his flesh burning, I heaved the eggs I'd eaten that morning in Snug Harbor right out onto the beach. Then I kicked sand and pebbles and seaweed over my sick, and kept on with the fire. Out near the blinking buoy, the phosphorescents bloomed in wide circles. The moon set. The tide flooded back out towards the North.

I heaped wood on the fire and stoked it all night long, and I hadn't brought a light, and Granddad's mess of a body caught and crackled and spit. I grasped for wood, my fingers churning into the the place I'd vomited, my hands numb and full of sand and splinters. All night I heaved wood onto the fire and Granddad's body smouldered and dripped, and the morning came. The sun struck me about the head. Island mornings are calm, kelp sails to shore with shrunken mermaid heads, terns wheel in the sky. Something was wrong.

Something was wrong with the fire. It was still going, if anything it was hotter than before, smoldering white all the way through the stacks of bark, the wind having helped me to stoke it through the night. Behind me, greasy black smoke coated the Island, settling down between all the trees over on Mosquito Pass, on Kellet's Bluff, where the eagles nested in the cliffs up from the empty fishermen's shanties, but Grandad was still there.

His clothes were burned, his skin was melted mostly off, he looked like black and red clay, but he didn't seem to be going anywhere. I was good at a lot of things, I was good at thumbing my nose, but what did I know about funeral pyres? Granddad told me what to do. He made me promise to burn him on the beach, but he didn't tell me how to do it. This was his dream, goddamnit, not mine. I tried, I tried my best to be an atheist. I could get in a lot of trouble for this. I could get anthrax. He wouldn't burn.

I shoveled on more wood. I set heavy white logs on top of the melted clay body. I threw rocks at it. I spat. I raged up and down the Storm Beach. I cursed. I cursed. I threw larger rocks. I threw the rocks that are speckled like baby seals, and the rocks with rings on them. I crushed crabs between rocks. I crammed a jellyfish in my mouth and tried to chew cartilage. Granddad's smell clothed me, thick and oily, his dead smell but his alive smell too. I loved that man. That randy bastard was making me sick. I shoveled on more wood. I threw it on in armfuls, not bothering to sort out the driftwood from its tangles of dried flotsam, so the seaweed with its pods of sticky sperm hissed and sprayed in the fire, turning the flames purple. I threw on armfuls of wood, and the day wore on, and

Granddad was still there, and I'll tell you one thing. He hadn't wanted it like this.

His muscle and sinew fried and scorched and fell from the bone, but his bones just leered at me, white and then charred, and they remained solid. And when the fire finally died, when I'd heaped on every bit of fuel I could find, I stood there spent, my eyes acrid and infected from the hours of smoke, my lungs full up with poison. His heart bubbled right up until the end, a fearsome fist of muscle and blood. Was it wrong that I thought of eating it? I'd had nothing since the ham and eggs with Virgil the previous morning, the remains of which lay speckled across my canvas shoes. I was hungry and I was in a vulnerable state of awe. I didn't actually do it, but still.

From among the ashes and debris, from among the signs of a struggle, I collected Granddad's bones. I balanced up the black rocks to the cape above the Storm Beach where I'd left the green wheelbarrow and I piled the bones in the wheelbarrow, and down at my feet I saw a glint of gold, and it was Granddad's wedding ring. It had fallen into a hill of red ants, and they swarmed over it, but I kicked dirt onto them, and some of them crawled into my shoes and stung me, and I scooped up the ring, and I put it in my pocket, and some of the ants were still on the ring, and they bit me above my nipple right through my woolen shirt, and as I pushed the wheelbarrow back into the woods, I passed the matted down places in the golden grass where the deer sleep before they leap up to run across the swamplands, so light as to leave only the small tracks a skipping stone might make. The sulphur smell off the swamp told me evening was coming so the tide would be changing again. And I pushed Granddad's bones through the forest.

I passed the place where, one summer when I was a boy, I dug a three foot deep booby trap. I wound my way to the back edge of the Island and I found the place where three white and silver-threaded stones stood, the Druid Stones, Granddad called them. He was relentless. He had wanted his ashes scattered here, but this would have to do. I dumped my wheelbarrow load, the dull bones clacking over one another. I didn't have a shovel, so I took up the moss in great sheets, and I spread it over the bones until I couldn't see them, and then I wiped my hands on my shirt, and the red ants bit me. My nose was streaming. It didn't matter that my eyes were streaming, but they were streaming, and I knew I would not leave the Island again. I knew I would stay with Grandmother. I would stay on the Island until the beautiful Island grew over me and I disappeared.

———

One night, towards the end of that winter we spent in the Wickiup, I came in for supper just as Grandmother was lighting the hurricane lantern. Granddad lay propped up in the lower bunk, leering at Grandmother and smoking cigarettes. I could tell they had just finished. I could tell she had just told him not to smoke inside. I could tell he would not leave her alone. She bustled around, clanging the meal together in a variety of cast iron skillets, her eyes dark as ever.

"Well, Edmond? Catch any selkies out there?" asked Granddad.

"Not tonight. But there were seal bones on the beach. The fox was in the high field."

"That fox. That old fox reminds me of someone."

"Only of yourself," said Grandmother.

"She hasn't stopped panting since the day I married her," said Granddad.

"Okay," I said.

"Edmond, why are you crying?" asked Grandmother. She put the tea kettle down, and came over to me and wrapped me around the waist. I could smell my Granddad on her.

"I'm leaving," I said. "That's why."

"Any idiot will always do what he likes," said Granddad. "Any goddamn idiot."

"Henry," said Grandmother.

"Shut your mouth, if you please, Colleen," said Granddad.

"I'm leaving the island," I said.

"As I said," said Granddad. He stubbed out his cigarette.

"Goddamn you," I said, "Don't you care about anything? I'm moving away." Granddad grinned and snorted.

"Where will you go?" asked Grandmother.

"Seattle," I said.

"Do you know anyone there, Edmond?" she asked. It was a way they had, of politely pretending that I had some secret grown-up life that they didn't know about, away from this fifty-acre island. That I might know people in Seattle that they didn't know. It was the way Granddad had of asking me, "Well Edmond?" when I'd got back from my afternoon walks, as if I had been out living my own life, maybe working odd hours at a delicatessen, or reading smutty novels, or scrounging up subway fare, or getting in a scuffle at a discotheque, or cheating on my pale vulgar wife with a thick-ankled teenager.

"I might know a few people in Seattle," I said. "I'll leave with Virgil in the morning."

"Virgil won't stop for you," Granddad said with relish, stretching his arms slowly over his head, and swinging his legs out over the side of the bunk. He sat on the edge of the bed in his thin underpants. He closed his eyes for a moment, scratching himself. "I'll take you in myself. You might want to go to Victoria though. Seattle, what do they have there? The streets there, Union Street, Third Avenue, full of men in mackinaws who couldn't find anything better to do with their lives than work it all away. Now, in Victoria—"

"Oh, yes," Grandmother said, "Henry took me there for our honeymoon. To the Empress Hotel."

"I sailed us there, in our old cabin cruiser, remember that, Colleen? You cooked our supper on the boat. Bangers and mash. Nothing fancy, and the hotel wasn't so grand as it is now. They enlisted me to fit the doors, and to build a small flight of wooden stairs to the dining room. I split a whole cord of shakes for the sauna they were putting in.

Then we sailed back to the Island. We were only gone two days. No bother. That's the way to do it."

"I'm not coming back to the Island," I said. "I might go to college."

"College. Well, you can always come back sometime soon," said Granddad.

"I wish you wouldn't go, Edmond," said Grandmother.

"You can always come back sometime soon. Just don't bother us about it too much," said Granddad. "I'll take you over in the skiff tomorrow. Dry your eyes, Edmond." He stalked out of the Wickiup, and I could hear his virile stream of urine against the spruce tree outside the door.

"He's torn up about your leaving, poor man," said Grandmother.

"Then why doesn't he say something about it," I said, "I don't like how he just sits and stares at me, then gets up and leaves."

"You're the one leaving, Edmond."

"Yes, Edmond," said Granddad, coming back in the door, "You're the one leaving. Just leave me to my own natural responses, if you please. I'm not you and you're not me. Can't help that." That's the way it was on the Island, everyone heard everything. To be delicate, one of us sometimes pretended to the other two that we were out of the room.

The following morning I arose early but saw that Granddad had woken earlier. My Grandmother snored into the space he'd left beside her in the bed, and I kissed her in a small way on her ear. I put my knapsack over my shoulder, and unearthed an ancient musty sleeping bag from the tool closet, disrupting a nest of mice. At the head of the dock, Granddad sat in the skiff, smoking, not bothering to look out into the straight where the water was choppy and capped in white. No matter, we'd make the crossing. Granddad wore no hat, and his iron colored hair streaked across his face in the wind. Grandmother'd be giving him his Spring haircut soon. He grinned at me as I came down the dock.

"Well, Edmond? What is it? We could just go, you and I, check the crab pots, and then come back home? How would you like that?"

"No, Granddad."

"Still leaving, are you, then?"

"Yes, Granddad."

He laughed. "Get in, then. Look to that bow line, why don't you?" I did.

We kept quiet on the crossing, and it was a hard crossing, the waves were high and they meant it, and the boat slammed down each time like we were landing on concrete, but we weren't worried, just contemplative about it.

Out past Open Bay, Granddad steered around the deadhead. At this tide it was hidden, but he went by memory anyway. Then the motor cut out, and the boat sputtered to nothing, just the slapping white caps, and our boat drifted sideways into the hills and valleys the ocean made. I cursed, but Granddad didn't curse. He just sat with his hands on his knees, looking out at Haro Straight, squaring his shoulders and pulling himself straight so that he looked like a rodeo rider while our boat tossed about on the swells. He didn't look at the motor. I said, "What's wrong with you? Why don't you choke it? Give it some fuel."

He said, "I was a boy in Cornwall when my street was bombed by the Germans. My mum and dad worked in the shipyard, you'll remember. If you looked up and up to the top deck of a man-o-war in dry dock you'd see just a chink of light. That was the sun, and down the street was a great hole where the school had been. We did our duty. We all did. My mum drew a line down the back of her legs, so that it would look like she was wearing stockings. On Sunday, I'd climb into my bed and my father'd bring me a tin mug of milk, and thick ham sandwiches, like no one anywhere was poor, least of all our family.

And then Mr. Churchill's voice came over the radio, we had it by the blacked-out window up in my bedroom where the reception was best, and my mum and dad and me—I'll never forget it. Shall I tell you what he said?"

"Tell me," I said.

"'We shall go on to the end, we shall fight in France, we shall fight on the seas and oceans, we shall fight with growing confidence and growing strength in the air, we shall defend our Island, whatever the cost may be, we shall fight on the beaches, we shall fight on the landing grounds, we shall fight in the fields and in the streets, we shall fight in the hills; we shall never surrender.'"

I sat in the bow, the salt spray dusting my face again and again, and the black gumdrop islands scattered before us, meeting the sky. They teemed with rioting life, deer, raccoons, plagues of rabbits whose populations roared up until they starved, otters, nameless twittering winter birds, all of them small, trying to get enough to eat, the soil full of salt.

"We shall fight them on the beaches," Granddad said, "Edmond, we shall fight them on the beaches," and his voice broke, and he crushed his head down into his hands and he sobbed.

———

When I was a boy on the Island, I worried each time I saw a lone seal pup, thinking that it had been abandoned, that its mother had been killed by poachers, men with no families who jettisoned trash into the ocean and cut through the water in mean silver boats. Grandmother came up over the cape one day, holding her canvas skirt above the dry island grass, and saw me edge towards a pup down on the Storm Beach, hand outstretched. "Edmond! Stop. Stop that. You'll make an orphan of that seal pup!" she cried to me quickly, her voice shrill on the wind, and I ran to her, humiliated, and butted my head gently against her. I was very small. "Its mother is only out hunting to feed it," she explained, "she'll be swimming back soon. You don't want to put a human smell on her pup. She'd abandon it." At the corner of Open Bay, coming in from Haro Straight, Granddad in the skiff was only a black spot.

FORT CLATSOP

My dad, Frank, and I were born on the same day forty years apart. On September seventh, 1988, I turned eleven and he turned fifty-one. At the Neskowin Laundromat, we looked at the daily newspaper, the horoscope section, to see what celebrity or historical figure we shared a birthday with. Frank ran his finger down the column. Our horoscope said we should keep our hopes high, but not too high, and not travel too far from home. "What a thing to tell a child and an old man," Frank shook his head. Besides that, the column did not list anyone at all whose birthday we shared, and I felt like crying. Frank ripped the paper up like it was nothing. "Screw these assholes. What do they know, Huck? Let me tell you, we share a birthday with one of the most honorable men ever born. Johnny Appleseed. Long after his traveling days were over, when he was an old man like I am now, I met him, and he told me everything he knew. He traveled around the country with a tin pan on his head. He planted apple trees and he peeked into people's windows. He wasn't such a jolly man as you might think, but he did have a mission. And having a mission is important."

Frank knew a lot of people personally, Johnny Appleseed was just one of them. But the way he told it, most of his crowd was long dead, and he was on his own now in a world of plain men and women. He was on his own, working as a janitor at Fire Valley Schoolhouse, in Neskowin, Oregon. It was the same job he'd had my whole life, and I was allowed to attend the school free of charge, along with the children whose clothing was woven in thick solid colors, whose hair was cut straight and chunky across their foreheads, who looked new and good against the misty sky and the grey green coast. At school potlucks, their parents said to each other, if the world ends today, and we are left with only each other, why that would be just about right.

Back in first grade, my dad was known for giving the best pushes on the tire swing of any of the other dads. Plus, the other kids were jealous that my dad got to spend all day with me, and even play ball with me at lunch if I wanted him to. But by the fifth grade it was clear that if your dad was the janitor, you were the janitor's kid, and anyway, where was your mother? Barry, the head teacher, said, "Hey, people. Let's call him a custodian okay? That makes Huck a custodian's daughter, not a janitor's daughter. Okay? Does that sound reasonable?" He tapped the peace gong quietly, to mark the moment. The peace gong was a xylophone.

Frank was truly in love with my mother, but I didn't remember her. When I asked, Frank told me she'd been captured by a motorcycle gang while I was still a baby. She'd written one postcard, he said, admitting she sort of liked the life, and Frank assured her we would be just fine on our own. Still, I could tell his feelings were hurt about it. During that summer before my sixth grade year, the small house I'd grown up in was finally condemned, and we found later that we'd left every picture of my mother inside when it was pulled to the ground. But I had never seen Frank without a plan.

"Huck," he told me while we stood together in the rubble, "I've found us a new place if you can keep quiet about it."

"Where is it?" I asked.

"It's not that we're going to do anything wrong, Huck, but the plain people, they might not understand. You won't be able to bring friends home, but I've never known you to bring friends home as it is."

Privately, I had planned for sixth grade to be different, but I said, "I can keep quiet, Frank."

The last night of July, we waited in the Beach Liner Diner until every last window on Main Street was dark. We climbed into the pick-up, and circled back to Fire Valley School. Frank used his keys to let us in a side door, and we stole down a back staircase into the bowels of the school, and through the small metal door into the boiler room. Frank had already outfitted the place with a couple of milk crates, a hot plate, his old army blanket.

Shoved back beneath a clanking steam pipe, a host of objects were sorted neatly onto a carpet of newspapers. Old computers, empty aquariums, record players, radios, and an oboe. All with the stenciled labels, "FVS."

"What's all that stuff? What are we going to do with an oboe?" I asked.

"Those are cast-offs, Huck," said Frank. "The school doesn't need them anymore, not the way we do. Trust me, Huck, they've got plenty of junk lying around. They won't even miss this stuff. You and me, Huck? We see things differently than the plain people do. To us, this stuff is not junk. No sir. This stuff can help us in our mission," said Frank. "Just leave it to me." I had hoped sixth grade could be different, but I saw now that nothing would ever be different. Or that Frank and I were already so different from other people that no other changes could matter.

All of August, I followed Frank through the deserted halls of Fire Valley Schoolhouse. I helped Frank chisel gum off of desks, wet down blackboards, and fill soap dispensers with the bubblegum pink powder that would cake our clean hands all year. In the evenings, we waited in the diner until it was safe to circle back to the school and let ourselves in the side door. We sat together in the boiler room, beneath pipes as thick as my body, I could hide in them if I only I could find a way in, and I helped Frank cover the "FVS" labels on the cast-off aquariums and computers. Weekly, Frank would load the pick-up, and take a trip to the pawn shop in Seaside. Sometimes I'd go with him, but more often, I liked to set a course into the woods out back of the school. If I pushed far enough through salal, blackberry, and ivy, through shingled coats of invasive species, if I walked and walked until the constant water from the undergrowth had soaked my thin clothing, I could turn around and look back and see the world as it truly was—pressing, dripping, lattices of green, with no trace of where I'd come from.

On September seventh, we sat on milk crates and ate birthday cake in the dark, whispering back and forth. The school clanked above us and the sounds were of ghosts up and down the hallways, and the next day, September eighth, was the first day of sixth grade. We were not allowed to have any lights except a candle. We were not allowed to speak at normal talking volume.

"Did Johnny Appleseed steal, those times that he peeked into people's windows?" I asked.

"He did what he had to do. He was real focused. He was focused on apples. Everyone should have such focus," Frank said.

When we still had the house, we had an oven and an electric range. Frank had specialized in making store bought foods from scratch, always with an imaginary crowd of people around him, telling him it couldn't be done. Frank would say, "This world is a wasteland sometimes, Huck. When you think about all those people out there who think graham crackers are something you buy in a box. Who owns graham crackers, Huck? No one. No one at all. You and I, Huck." He'd bring his sheet of home made graham crackers out of the oven, and I'd eat them warm while he shook his fists at the imaginary crowd and slapped his knees in triumph. "What did I tell you? Don't tell me what I can and cannot do." Frank also made oreo cookies, mayonnaise, spaghetti noodles, and jell-o. He made twinkies with particular glee.

By candlelight, we ate store-bought cake in the boiler room, and Frank told me again about being a hobo with Frying Pan Jack, Woodie Guthrie, and the others. For our birthday dinner, he'd boiled mulligan stew over our hot plate. Mulligan stew could be made with a boot, Frank said, but luckily we had cream of broccoli and a can of black beans to put in it. We had a pot. We had two spoons. We had the cake like a yellow sponge between us. Frank's voice had risen while he talked and a dog barked from the neighboring property. Frank blew out the candle and we sat silently in the dark.

The sixth grade got to have class in the barn. The floors were hard wood, and the place was insulated now, but we got to sit on bales of straw. Barry introduced us to Alan, the new kid, a very small boy with black freckles. "Tell us where you're from, Alan," said Barry.

"Alfirk," said Alan and looked straight up. Barry laughed. "Welcome, Alan, welcome. As you can see we're roughing it out here in the barn." Barry clapped his hands together and addressed the entire class, pushing Alan gently towards one of the straw bales. "But that's how it's going to be in the sixth grade. You're the oldest in the school.

You're about to go out and meet the world and bring the message of Fire Valley Schoolhouse far and wide, and you know how that makes me feel?"

Barry paused, and breathed deeply with his mouth closed. His cheeks shone. "Of course you know. Very, very proud. We've got a special way of life here at Fire Valley, and I think sitting on straw bales is a big part of that. Just think how this world would be if every man, woman, and child had a chance to sit on straw bales instead of driving in cars. That's what I'm talking about. Okay people, let's get started."

Barry said we were going to build a life sized model of Fort Clatsop. He showed us some photographs of the real thing, and said we could take a field trip there as part of our research, because that's what sixth graders did, research. He showed us a shadowy photo of a little wooden bed. He said, "Take a look at this. Sacajewea slept here, along with her boozy husband, Charbonneau, the Frenchman. Do you notice anything about this bed? That's right. It's very small. And can anyone tell me why it's so small?"

I raised my hand. Barry looked at me and raised his eyebrows.

"People were smaller back then," I said.

"Well, yes," Barry said slowly, "that's evident. But why?"

"They were starving," I said, "just starving to death. Not much food." I remembered it the way Frank had told it to me, "People began to get smaller and more efficient, they—"

"Frances," said Barry.

"Huck," I corrected him.

"Frances Huckleberry Simms," he said, taking a little bow. The class laughed. "If you think about what you've said, I believe you'll realize just how little sense it makes."

"No, really, it's true."

"Okay, people," Barry was calm and reasonable like always, "Can anyone tell me why people were so small?" He paused. "That's right. The answer is that no one knows. The greatest men in science do not know, and Frances Huckleberry Simms also does not know." The class laughed. Barry sat down on the straw bale he used as his desk. He waited for the laughter to die down. He stroked his chin. He spoke quietly. "You know something? Sometimes it takes a big person to just say, 'Hey—I don't know.' Three words. But they mean a lot." Barry touched the peace gong softly.

At lunch, the new kid Alan came up to me where I sat by myself at one of the log picnic tables near the edge of the woods. He wiped his nose angrily on his sleeve.

"Is it true what you were saying about people being smaller?" He asked me in a damp voice.

"Of course it's true. That's actually one reason you hear stories now about people hiding behind things, and sometimes you think, how could they have hidden behind a barrel, say, or a bunch of ferns, or a rock, and not be found. Like I said, people were smaller. Animals, too. Even today you can see deer like dogs." We looked around us, for modern day evidence, but all we saw was Frank, lifting a garbage can by the corner of the black top. He saw us too, and waved.

"The janitor here has no teeth," said Alan.

"That's Frank. He's my dad," I said.

"How come your dad doesn't have any teeth?" Alan asked. His mouth hung open when he was done talking, and he kept glancing up at the sky.

"They fell out when he was in the army," I said. "He fought alongside Elvis Presley in the Korean war."

"Elvis who?"

"Where did you say you were from?"

Alan glanced down from the sky at me for a second. You could see he was pleased. "Alfirk."

"Where's that?"

"It's a star."

"Like in outer space?"

"Yes. Six hundred light years away."

"So you're an alien."

"Yes. That's why I can neither read nor write, and also, I have special powers."

"Like what?"

"I can tell the future and I have what they call photographic memory, and also some other things."

"Yesterday was my birthday," I told Alan. I could see he made trouble, but mostly in quiet ways, so that people thought, he's not making trouble, he's just one of those lonely kids. But really he was making trouble.

"Happy birthday," he said.

Back in class, Barry had an announcement. "You all know Frank Simms, Frances's dad. He's been the custodian here since 1977. He's a hard worker and a good man. The other teachers and I were lounging around the teachers' lounge yesterday, where we have unlimited access to chocolate milk. And what did we think? That's right. We thought, hey—wait a minute now—wasn't it Frank's birthday yesterday? Well, what a perfect time to give old Frank a good old thank you. So, let's all pitch in and see if each and every student in this school can't make Frank a birthday card. The theme will be 'I want to be a janitor when I grow up because…' you fill in the blank of course. Let's have these done by Friday, alright?"

One of the girls in a chunky wool sweater and clogs raised her hand.

"What if you don't want to be a janitor when you grow up?" she asked. A few people laughed. Barry laughed too. Then he grew solemn, and closed his eyes.

"Martin Luther King Jr. had a message for the world," he said quietly, "and that message was to be the best street sweeper you can be. Which I take to mean that sometimes it's okay to pretend you want to be a street sweeper, or in this case a janitor, if it's going to make that certain janitor look at his life and maybe, just once, feel proud of himself, feel that he can be—if not the president of the United States or even the Secretary of State—well at least he can be the best street sweeper or janitor he can possibly be. Do you understand that? We are going to give Frank a gift, and I think Frank needs a gift. Does that sound reasonable?" The class nodded. Barry opened his eyes. "Great, people, I knew I could count on you. Okay, back to Fort Clatsop. Now, if you're like me you always thought 'Meriweather' was a girl's name, but boy were you wrong."

In the boiler room that night, Frank dipped a brush in black paint from the art room, and carefully applied it to the label on a violin case. I told him all about Fort Clatsop. "The main thing is that Lewis and Clark didn't have it so easy. They moved in on Christmas Eve and stayed there all winter. But they made a ton of jerky, and they shot flintlock rifles, and muskets, and made fires from flint and steel, and they made a dugout canoe, and the Clatsop Indians taught them to make moccasins. They remade their maps, and revised their journals, and started back for St. Louis in the spring."

Frank took out a permanent marker and began to fill in the white stenciled initials on the black rim of an overhead projector. He was pretty good at it. You couldn't even tell what it used to say. Tomorrow was Frank's day off, and he was due for another trip to Seaside.

"Things have changed a lot since those days," said Frank. "I mean, look at us. We're warm, we're dry, our beds are the right size." Frank didn't have a bed, unless you counted his old army blanket, and I just had a mattress in the corner, but I still got his general point. "But some things are the same. Take you and me, for instance. We may not be building a dugout canoe, but we're planning, planning all the time. We've got a mission and we've got focus. Also, I might mention that if we had to make jerky, we certainly could."

Frank moved with his marker to a cassette player, which was new to the collection. "Huck, I've got something to tell you. We're getting out of this boiler room. I've got a sure fire plan. I've been doing a lot of thinking, and I'm going to start my own business. I'm going to make home made cornflakes from scratch, and maybe some corn crispies too, or corn-O's, I mean I figure once I've got the recipe down, I can make pretty much any shape cereal I want to. Now, they'll tell you that cereal can only be made in a factory, but you can't listen to them. That's the key to our success. You see, you can't even find a recipe for cereal anywhere, and trust me, I've been looking. So the way I see it, I patent my own, I start producing it, and it catches on so fast, we'll be out of here by Christmas, easy."

"I made a friend today," I said, but my dad didn't answer, and the way it was so dark and so desperate, I couldn't tell whether or not he had heard me say it.

Alan came up to me the next day at lunch. "You didn't tell me you and your dad have the same birthday," he accused me, looking at the sky.

"If you were really psychic, you would have known," I said.

"I'm not actually psychic so much as I can tell the future."

"Oh, yeah, like what can you tell?"

He glanced down at me. "Well, like for instance, I can tell that you'll be really beautiful when you grow up."

"Shut up."

"No, really." Alan frowned at me, then again at the sky. "You'll be beautiful from straight on, and also from the right side. Unfortunately the left side of your face will look like you were the victim of a slight stroke."

"Ha. Very funny."

"It's not funny." Alan wiped his nose on his sleeve again. "Just before I left Alfirk, my mom had a stroke. She's in a nursing home now."

"So, I'm going to have a stroke?"

"No, you'll just be a little funny looking."

"Well, you're funny looking now."

"Yeah." We sat in silence for a while.

"So if your mom had a stroke, where do you live now?" I asked.

"I have to live here on your earth. With my aunt," Alan said.

"What does she think of Alfirk?"

"She won't let me talk about home," he said.

Across the playground, a boy in checkered overalls and a crocheted cap yelled at us, "HUCK AND ALIEN BOY, SITTING IN A TREE, K-I-S-S-I-N-G!" I hunched into my jacket and waited for Alan to leave, but instead he sat down next to me and pulled out a bag of M&Ms. He opened it and took out two, a red one and a yellow one. He put one M&M in each palm and closed his fists around them. He held out his fists. "Pick one."

I picked his right fist. Inside was the yellow M&M. "Everyone here thinks being a sixth grader means something really big," he said. "They act like this school was their own spaceship and they were happy about it. But they'll die lonely."

"What?"

"Pick the other one." I touched his left fist. Inside was the red M&M.

"Okay, they'll divorce, and then die lonely," he said.

"What about us? What will happen to us?" I asked. But Alan watched the M&Ms melt into his hands. He wiped them on his jeans. He sighed and closed his eyes.

"What did you and your dad do for your birthday?" He asked, "Did you have a party?"

The hot plate, the canned beans, the army blanket.

"A party where?"

"Where you live."

The stolen oboe, the stolen aquarium, the pawn shop.

"We live in the boiler room," I said and held my breath.

"Can I come over some time?" Alan asked.

The long nights in the Beach Liner Diner, waiting until it was safe to circle around back to the school basement. The weekends in the Neskowin Laundromat. The stories about the old times that did not mean a thing anymore. The cereal factory.

"Sure. Come on over today after school." I told myself the damage was done.

When the students thronged past us at the final bell, I nodded to Alan. "You have to be quick and follow me," I said, and we swerved down the back stairs to the basement. Under cover of the elephant thunder above our heads, I led Alan through the steel door into our camp. He stood near the entrance, taking in everything in the humming low room. We listened to the tocking pipes, the dripping coming from somewhere in the shadows. Alan came slowly forward and sat down on a milk crate.

"You can't live here forever," he said, "someone is going to find out and then you'll go to jail." The hurt of my mistake shocked hot tears into my eyes, burned my throat closed, but it served me right. It served me right to think I had anything in common with anyone still living, anyone except Frank.

"You're not like us," I struggled to say. "You're not our kind of people. Frank and I have our own crowd, only they're mostly dead by now."

"Like who?" asked Alan, peering at me with genuine curiosity.

"You wouldn't know them. You didn't even know who Elvis Presley was."

"I might know them," said Alan.

"Wyatt Earp? Crazy Horse? Mother Jones? Agatha Christie?" I began challenging him, but it was hard to explain. It was hard to explain that these were our talismans, our measure of the brightness that had occurred, that could occur again. This was our carefully tended archive of what it could mean to never fit in anywhere. I wanted Alan to leave. I wanted to go out, alone again, and set a course for where it was green.

"I am like that," Alan interrupted me.

"What?"

"I'm like that too. You asked what will happen to us. Well, think about it. We're like Lewis and Clark, only most people around here don't know it," he said.

"Then why did you say they'd find out? Why did you say we're going to jail?" I asked.

"Because it's true. You can't stay here," said Alan. "And I can't stay where I am either. I just wanted to make sure. We have to find someplace else."

"Like a mission?" I asked.

"Yes," said Alan. "Yes, like a mission."

On Friday morning, we filled the Multi Room. Barry stood up front. Once we were all quiet, he went to the door. "Frank!" He called to my dad. Outside the window, we watched Frank push a large broom against the perimeter of the building, mouthing words to himself. "Frank!" called Barry again, and my dad looked up. He smiled a gaping toothless smile. "Come on in here, Frank!" Barry beckoned Frank into the building. My dad stepped into the room and blinked at the students all lined up in rows with red downy cheeks. He took his hat off, and ran his hand over his face. He squinted around to find me, and when he found me, he waved hello like there was still a pane of glass between us, like there wasn't anyone else there anyway. Then he stood there, holding his hat, waiting for Barry to tell him what to do next.

"It's people like Frank who built this country." Barry began, "If it were up to Frank every man would know what it feels like to sweat, to complete an honest day's work. At Fire Valley School we give Frank the opportunity to be a respected laborer. Out in the real world, of course, it's a very different picture. But there are some people who have a better idea, the idea of equality. The idea that every man owns his own labor. The idea that we can divide the land, the food, the labor, and the women equally between all people according to one's need and ability. Such a man is Frank Simms. Happy Birthday Frank. Happy Birthday." My dad kept smiling, but his eyes moved all around, and I feel he already knew he was caught in a trap. One by one, the students of Fire Valley Schoolhouse stepped forward and read their cards aloud.

"I want to be a janitor when I grow up because you would be able to rescue balls off the roof."

"Custodian," said Barry.

"I want to be a janitor when I grow up because I hate it when my mom makes me take a bath."

"Custodian," said Barry.

"I want to be a custodian when I grow up because it would be a lot better than being a street sweeper."

"Street Cleaner," said Barry. Alan was next.

"I want to be a janitor when I grow up..." he began.

"Custodian," said Barry.

"Custodian. I want to be a custodian when I grow up because then I could collect all kinds of old stuff the school doesn't want anymore, and sell it at the pawn shop with Frank. I could live in the boiler room with Frank and Huck," said Alan, and he widened his eyes at me across the room, and he smiled, and I hadn't known it would be like this, but I couldn't help it. I smiled back.

For a moment it seemed that no one would believe him anyway, the way the room just stayed put, Barry with his tiny wooden mallet half raised towards the peace gong. But before anyone could decide to make a move, like he couldn't stop himself, Frank looked at me and said, "Is this your new friend? Huck, my Huck. You ain't got the sense you was born with." He just gave it all up, and Barry stood there like he could hardly believe it, but then like maybe he could. It was not in our nature to deny things.

I pushed forward, through the crowd of people, past the wheaty girls and wind blown boys, past Barry whose jaw was dropping as he fumbled for the telephone. I could hear it all falling apart louder now, and policemen throwing light into the darkest corners of our house. We wouldn't need the army blanket, or even the tin pot to wear like a helmet. I pushed through the crowd to the front of the room. Alan took my arm. "Let's go," he said, and he grasped my bewildered father's hand. Alan and I got Frank out the door, and we pulled him towards our old truck. His mouth hung open, and he didn't put up much resistance when we pushed him into the driver's seat and climbed into the cab behind him. Frank only needed a little coaxing to start up the truck and pull on out of there.

"Alan? Why didn't you wait so we could plan this together? What if they follow us?" I asked. But it was Frank who spoke next.

"Huck, you don't trust me anymore, that must be it. Our whole mission, down the drain, and now we're on the lam. Ah, Huck. How could you give up on me this way?"

When he asked me, I knew. I knew what was on Alan's mind, and I told it to Frank the way that it arrived whole inside me. The boiler room, the oboes and aquariums, the pawn shop. Those are not part of our mission, is what I explained to Frank. Living that way is only evasion, and it's imaginable to the plain people. It's a form of resistance they can understand and eradicate. They can laugh at it. They can catch you. It's small time. It's a compromise where there can be no compromise. What is left to us? To live in such a luminous way that anyone who tries to trace us is blinded.

We could do almost anything, I explained to my dad, we could make almost anything ourselves. We could work hard for a season, far away from the plain men and women, out in the wet still layers of the mystery woods. We could make M&Ms, a spaceship, almost anything.

"Where are you from, son?" My dad asked Alan, as he pulled onto the highway, and the woods were dripping and pretty nearby the waves were crashing.

"Alfirk," said Alan.

"Oh, yes, my wife's people were from around that area, I believe."

Alan and I looked at each other. After that, it was only a matter of time before we realized that Alan was not an alien from outer space, but something more strange and wonderful. He was my twin. We had been separated at birth, but now we were reunited. All that long winter, as we hunted with our muskets, and made jerky and sewed together buckskin breeches, and built fires without matches, and split logs and carved our dugout canoe for the unfathomable trip, we pieced it together.

A SOW ON THE LAM

A sow, on the lam, makes for the forest and bears a litter in the leaves. She lives out her curious life among the roots of tulip poplars, coarse hollow stems of Cohosh, and strings of Goldenseal, obstinate Greenbriar, and all the common ferment. That sow is slumming it. But no matter. She bore her piglets in the wild, and only two generations later, her grandchildren will be feral, with tusks, with coarse yellow-tipped manes, with long bristling whiskers. But these feral pigs are not as wild as deer, and I am a scientist. In the places I know, in woods and along the shore, deer have been wild as long as their history. Real deer history began when the deer were outside and had no inside to go to. Then their eyes, previously as expressive as our own, became impenetrable, dark, dark and uncomprehending. Maddeningly wild, and they remain so. If you lived in a field, in the woods, along the shore, with no hut like the hut you have, if you moved all day without the expectation of cooked food in the evening, without a warm close place to recline in and to eventually experience a certain listlessness, you would become a deer, too. But that's a story, and as I have said, I am a scientist.

By now, you and every other radio listener know that the Copes-Brinkley Mud Turtle finally achieved extinction. But in that final harsh summer, I went to its region to study the Copes-Brinkley, and, though I hesitate now to suggest this, to save it. I set up in the derelict fried chicken stand, coolers and sediment, specimens, slides. A radio with a handle to crank power into it when the green light came on.

Each morning, I rose before it was light, and I drove my lemon out to the beach ditch where the final host of Copes-Brinkley had been spotted, roosting in the offal. They didn't care, because they were alive. They were in the middle of their personal lifetime, so they roosted in the offal like all Copes-Brinkley had always done, huddling in their dark brittle shells, unaware. I would have liked them to feel the urgent link to their ancestors and progeny, to their region and habitat. But I could not make them feel it. I drove, though nothing now could be done for the Copes-Brinkley. I would be the one to do it.

The families in the region had all been pig farmers, I learned at the Carnegie library, open by appointment on the main street of that ghost town. But the indestructible hog concerns moved in and bought up every small farm back in the hollows, in the spiny deciduous woods along the lake, the ditches caked with clay, the Copes-Brinkley habitat. Compare a pig farm to an industrial hog farm. It's like composing a poem for someone, then handing it to them along with the pamphlet that came in the box with your microwave. You could say they're both writing.

The hog concerns cooked up vast monocrops of stench. You may adhere to science all you want. I do. I am a scientist. Yet the smell of an industrial hog farm surpasses science. It is unprovable. It is religious.

After the stench, the runoff began, first leaking in rivulets from the hog farms, followed by mud slides and luges of shit and fat, hog sludge draining into the ditches, where the Copes-Brinkley dutifully dug their tunnels, brummated through each winter just below the frozen slime.

The Copes-Brinkley didn't know what was good for them. They liked the hog sludge! They liked it but it was killing them! They'd come up because it got hot, stop breathing through their tails, stop brummating, surface and freeze overnight. Forgive me, but where's the self-preservation in that? Next, the hogs began to escape the farms. Only a few of them per year, but that was enough. Every nine months they bear a brood, generations go by quickly, and wild hogs were grinding their cloven hooves into the Copes-Brinkley habitat, rooting with their tusks, destroying the Copes-Brinkley tunnels, and the turtles didn't even have the good sense to cower.

So you see, for the Copes-Brinkley, the problem was many pronged. The hog farms, the sludge, the feral pigs. The coyote and the raven ate up what leftovers they could. The Copes-Brinkley moved snout down, sucking up all food, and so their eggs were marbled with particles, the babies were oily. What can it mean to live like that? In a shell. I came to resent it. The difference between the Copes-Brinkley and almost everything else is that its shell was black. It needed water and black grime. It's not something we can ever hope to empathize with, the radio journalist later asserted, and I was pissed.

The radio journalist called in early June, when I thought it was humid because I didn't yet know what humid could be. She left a message on my TracFone in the fried chicken stand. Public Radio wanted to air a story about the Copes-Brinkley, said the journalist. She put it to me like this: Why should anyone care about the Copes-Brinkley? I bridled at the blinking machine, moved to press erase, but she said, Wait! We're really asking! We really want to give you a chance to tell people why they should care! We're going to give you time to explain. Look, she said, This is long form. Actually, it will probably be a series.

I sat on my cot in my undershirt. I played and replayed the message. The backs of my legs stuck to the mattress.

The hog concerns themselves had shown no interest in my comings and goings. They were unflappable in the face of possible litigation, and did not worry about my research. In fact, they sent me a note on industry letterhead to say they wished me luck in saving the Copes-Brinkley, and that they were all for sustainability. Cynical, yes, though even this was more than I'd heard from any of my colleagues.

Beside me was the shotgun I'd bought so I could shoot a feral pig if it came to that, which was not in my job description, but was its own honest category. Previous to this, I had not shot a gun or even held one, but the research I did at the Carnegie Library told me that it would not be the most difficult thing I had ever done, and that, in fact, people like me held and shot guns every day for a variety of reasons, desperate or not. My research told me to mind the kickback, and that the most skillful way to set your iron sights is with both eyes open.

I replayed the journalist's message. I called her back. I told her my job was to monitor the Copes-Brinkley, not to interfere. To watch, wait, and record. To tag, I told her.

Are you a public radio listener? She asked me.

I told her I was a member. I had a tote bag. I had a mug. I had Carl Kasell's voice on my home answering machine. I wanted it to be Terry Gross, but the journalist said, Terry doesn't leave the studio. I hoped for Lakshmi Singh, but the journalist said, Lakshmi is overseas, even now she is peering around the corners of buildings. I'm very good at my job, she said. I'm someone who asks the right questions. I coax people to say what they mean, which is what's needed now.

Where I was, there was no local affiliate. I told the journalist I was available every day, all day long, and on weekends, and in the evenings, and in the early mornings, and on the fourth of July. I told her that she was welcome to follow the Copes-Brinkley and me around all she wanted. Excellent, she said. I'll be there soon. You just keep doing your good work. And think of some answers while you're at it. I want to know all about that turtle. I really do! You watch out, you'll get tired of me, she said. You see if you don't!

So I drove. The backseat stacked with my paraphernalia, beakers, tanks, thermometers, I drove to the habitat each morning. I monitored, I tagged, I wrote dire reports. All of June, I thought I might career into a giant piece of flora. I left my 12 gauge stowed in the trunk under a canvas tarp, and I waited for the journalist.

And each morning, I woke like a cabbage folded way down in the pickle jar, a rat of bone and hair, wetted down. Never like a person someone would want to stay longer in bed with, never like a person someone else would decide to ignore the alarm for. That's what the Copes-Brinkley had done to me. I was alone with the animal. Each day was a perfect day for the journalist to arrive, but each day she did not arrive and soon it was July.

In July, I parked beneath the sycamore, just outside the habitat patch, then picked along the track to the beach ditch, only this time there was a boy. There was a boy, hunched down in the sludge, scooping tunnels in the mud with the help of a blunt root he'd torn free from a bare-knobbed sassafras. A boy in the habitat. I stepped towards him, ready to shoo him, but he straightened and saw me. "I'm digging," he said. I took him for twelve when his voice quavered bravely between octaves, and he had that screw-eyed look peculiar to those who don't expect to be seen. He wore mud splattered spectacles, a windbreaker, the wrong shoes.

"What are you doing in the habitat?" I asked.

"I'm digging," he repeated.

"You'll have to lay off that," I said.

"Why? I dig a tunnel and the turtles crawl through it. They like it. They want me to do it. They don't care what you think."

"I'm trying to save the Copes-Brinkley," I said.

"What's that?" the kid said.

"That's the proper name of the turtle," I said.

"How do you know?"

"I'm a marine biologist," I said.

"I've been watching you," he said, "and all you do is watch them."

"I'm monitoring," I said. "Digging tunnels for them doesn't help. They need to dig their own tunnels. And I don't only watch them. I tag them."

"I could help you do that. I can catch things without scaring them," said the kid, peering into the mud. I considered this, and did some rapid math. It was just the blackened indifferent animal and me and, way off in the distance, the churning of a damned tractor. The habitat was devastated and now there was a boy in it.

"Can I get you something?" the kid said. "What do you like to eat? I could get it for you."

"Do you live around here?" I asked.

"My father has a farm up the road there, on the south face of the hill."

"I thought all the families left this area," I said. "I thought there was no one left."

"My father doesn't mind the smell," the boy said.

"What about your mother?" I said.

"Oh, my mother," the boy said. "She's around here somewhere. She's probably driving a pig to forage."

"We have to do things in a professional way because a journalist is coming," I said. "She has taken an interest. She is planning a radio story and I don't want anything to get in the way of that."

"But I won't be in the way. I'll help."

I thought about it.

"Just until the journalist gets here," I said. "Then, I'll do the talking. This isn't a cute kid thing. It's about endangered species."

"I'm not cute," the boy said, and this was true.

His name was Andy and I set him to work making sandwiches because that's proper for an intern, which is what I decided he must be after I read some scientific journals I had lying around my lab. Poor nutrition was responsible for the behavior of many moody characters in canonical literature, mostly American. Andy, I could see, brooded and worse, he felt no sincere empathy for the animal. To him, the Copes-Brinkley was just a pastime. He was making a childhood memory out of the whole struggle. I ground my teeth in the beach ditch and Andy could hear it. But we worked side by side. He made sandwiches in the morning and put them in the cooler. He kept a notebook of his own. I told him some data but I'm not certain that he wrote it down. I never saw either of his parents. I noticed that he did not know how to use a can opener. I made him a present of some pudding, and another day, some graph paper.

I tried to explain to Andy important things such as the web of life, such as seven generations, such as riparian. I knew his people were pig farmers and I hoped to impress upon him: In two generations, a passel of hogs becomes a sounder of wild pigs. Wild! Behold their back bristles standing on end, their tusks, three inches of ivory. They may carry a stripe across their shoulders, a telltale mark of their ancestral domesticity, but make no mistake: they will snap your arm in two with their jaws. They will run amok through your habitat unless you are vigilant, and the Copes-Brinkley are vigilant about nothing but brummating.

But these words did not come, as we squatted in the beach ditch side by side, though Andy watched me avidly, hoping for meaning in all of it. But what could I say? He had been submerged in that dark tangle all his growing up years, had been kept home to help with the failing farm, and did not know other children. The entire habitat was the same dripping color. Mossy sludge, ticking, whirring, smooth sinister trunks, branches, vines, all encased in tunnels of muddy bark, inches deep. Through its lattice, the yellow sky sometimes, but we were down so low it hardly seemed to matter. "I live in a clearing," Andy once told me. "Just so you know."

Andy did not go to school or summer school or play sports. He knew many fallen trees that sprung strangely so that he could make a game of bouncing on them to make them swing him into the air.

During these dog days, I was not sleeping well, partly due to tap tapping of mice and ricocheting of bats. These were of a species whose families were doing well, though they had predators whose families were also doing well.

Andy did not have a friend even though he said he did. Neither did I though I did not talk much about it. The other marine biologists had long ago turned from me in shame. They were impotent or I was. The other marine biologists wouldn't touch the Copes-Brinkley, not one. They never liked the animal because the animal lived mostly in the mud, which made the word "marine" seem as far away as a menacing low tide, in the distance you could see it but it left yards of stink and sand behind. No marine biologist wants to go up against a hog farm if they don't have to. There was the smell, and also the obvious question—what does a hog have to do with the sea? The Copes-Brinkley Mud Turtle was barely admissable in the field of marine-biology, but it was my niche.

"It's good for a boy to have friends his own age," I suggested in deep July, as Andy handed me a cress sandwich from the cooler. He produced a plastic fringed wallet from the back pocket of his cutoffs, and he opened it to show me a picture of himself. It must have been himself. It looked just like him, though I could see that he had drawn freckles on the photo with a ballpoint pen. "You?" I asked. "That's my best friend, Buck," he said. "He doesn't live around here no more but I used to see him every day." I could not say if he meant it for a joke. I laughed anyway, and he said, "Yeah, those Cokes-Binkey, they laugh too."

"Copes-Brinkley don't laugh," I said.

"Ha. That's what you think," he said. "They laugh by chuffing."

"No, they don't," I said.

"Scientist," he said, as a slur. But we ate sandwiches dripping with mayonnaise and some human hair. We worked together and waited for the journalist.

Waiting, it came to me that I could be a radio panelist for the Copes-Brinkley, speaking into the microphone alongside my colleagues. But then I remembered, what colleagues? Who would consent to be on a panel with me? Andy? He was like an animal of the field because he ate cold stew or whatever was around, raw potatoes, whatever. His eyes would scan and not reflect, so you knew he might not understand human things. This might seem like good luck, but it is bad luck.

Andy taught me his favorite game, Survival of the Fittest Stick.

"It's what it sounds like," he said. "You hit a stick against another stick to see which stick breaks. Then, you take the winning stick and hit it against a different stick." I could see what was to come. Andy would eventually work his way up to the strongest stick in the forest.

At the end of each day, Andy hid the champion stick amid other sticks that looked like it. This was so that no one would notice the special stick and steal it. From his father, Andy had learned to mark wild ginseng patches with decayed box elder, skewed to one side, to signify morels by a broken twist of grass. There will always be those whose work it is to recognize your signs. The work of your life is to foil them.

At the brink of August, Andy said, "My mother says hello, can she get you anything, and am I being a nuisance." A Copes-Brinkley cow tunneled deeper. Her egg bubbled. I fingered my wax pencil.

"Where's your mother?" I asked.

"Up the road in the clearing. I saw her swearing at the water pump this morning. Something stuck I guess. But it'll flush out."

"I could meet her sometime if she can come down here," I said.

"We'll see what my dad says."

"It's like that?"

"My dad's been up in the hills the past few days. Storming most likely. "

"Storming?"

"Be back soon I guess."

I took his mother for a meek woman but figured that's their culture. Or figured, I'd better keep to my niche. I'd never been very good at talking to people. Still, the journalist did not come.

Andy often met me in the morning as if he hadn't slept at all, his mood unchanged by early or late hours, his spectacles misting over until he wiped them abstractedly on his cutoffs. He sat on a stump or kicked pebbles into the beach ditch no matter the time or heat of the day. But one morning, I arrived at the habitat, and Andy wasn't there.

I parked under the sycamore, and I went forward into the habitat alone. I squatted down on the embankment to catch the early morning tunneling of the animal, the way their jet eyes surface, suspicious and flinty, unlidded each day. The suffocating cloud that sank down into the dawn habitat began to lift away, and I could see into the primary Copes-Brinkley roost. Through the tunnel opening I saw the younger cow. She moved so that I could see her hind quarters struggling in the mud. She had a strange mark upon her. It was a tag. It was not my tag. It was a tag tagged by someone else. I was stunned.

Then a motor. Then I turned around, and the journalist, for it could only be the journalist, at last clambering out of her car such like, watching her boots suck down into habitat mud, and they were not boots made for that sort of contact, I could see. I drew myself up. She examined her boots. I waited.

I waited, and though my regard for public radio borders on the slavish, I was in that moment overcome with what I can only call my buried doubts about the medium. With radio you must ask people to use their imaginations, and I was prepared to do that. In earnest broadcast, I would ask people around the nation to imagine the Copes-Brinkley, their condition, their slick beach ditch, their black shells, the oily eggs, the sludge, the winter that faithfully rolled frost onto their tunnels but they provided their own insulation and came out each spring unmarred. The trouble with radio is that you ask people to use their imaginations, but after that, you don't hear back.

Radio journalists may be generous or cavalier, they may be overtaken by a holiday feeling, and when that happens, they may describe what they are wearing. They might say they are wearing an oversized angora sweater. The sweater is the color of charcoal, they might say, and they are wearing that sweater over slacks. The slacks are of a matching hue. But, they explain, the ensemble is not entirely monochrome, because—and here the journalists are almost shy—they are wearing red boots. I had heard public radio journalists describe themselves thus countless times, usually during pledge drives, or first thing in the morning. Yet for all I knew, they were naked.

That was the trouble with radio. There was so much to be suspicious about, and so much generosity. I wore a windbreaker, waders, and kevlar trousers, like I did that whole season with the Copes-Brinkley, sweating inside of my getup if that's what the situation called for. I was intrepid. I looked at the journalist, orienting herself in the habitat, and I saw that she wore exactly what she had described herself wearing on air. I was overcome with terror and dread.

Yet I did not let it show. I watched the journalist accept that her red boots were muddy. I watched her lift her head and register the relentless reeking oily scent of the hog farms. It was especially heavy in the morning fog, coating the habitat in greasy cologne. The journalist caught her breath against the smell and came towards me along the narrow swathe of road. Her hair was enviable like a shaggy goat, a shock of white along one side, otherwise dark. A barrette held it back from her endless forehead.

"So you're the hero of the Copes-Brinkley Mud Turtle," she said. We shook. Her teeth were enormous and evenly spaced. She put her hand on a notebook peeking out of her hip pocket.

"I wouldn't put it like that," I said, but I was flustered.

"Then how would you put it?"

"I'm a scientist," I said.

"And I'm a journalist," she said.

"I know," I said.

"What exactly is that disgusting smell?" she asked. "My god. I can't believe you can work here."

"Several hundred chemicals make up the smell of a hog farm," I blurted, "Volatile fatty acid groups, gaseous dust emissions. Your throat is scratchy, your chest is tight, you can't even drink water without gagging. All this, and no provable ill health effects to stake a claim on."

"Is that what's threatening the Copes-Brinkley?" The journalist asked. She pinched her nose, "Is it the unbearable smell?"

"Are you kidding? The only ones who don't mind the stench are the Copes-Brinkley, and I hate them for it."

"You hate the Copes-Brinkley?" she asked quickly, pulling out her notebook.

"I care about them."

"Of course," she said, lowering her notebook again. "That's why I'm here. What do you do here at the site, exactly?" Her eyes watered.

"We monitor," I told her again.

It's true that I was not the hero of the Copes-Brinkley Mud Turtle. But sometimes two people fall in love, can they help it? Fifty years on, one of the lovers begins to fail. And in their grief, the non-failing partner begins to be angry at the failing one. How could you do this? Be like you were! Get over this and be yourself again! In the final months of my grandfather's life, my grandmother raced ahead of him down the sidewalk. She'd make it to the street corner long before him, then turn back and yell, We don't have all day here! My grandfather, unable to answer, degenerating into a quiet wispy death, tottered along behind her. My grandmother's anger was the most vital thing going. And that's how it was with me and the blasted Copes-Brinkley.

"They lay eggs out their cloacas," I told the journalist bitterly.

"Is that a fact," she said.

"That's science," I said. "Don't ask me why."

The journalist wasn't looking at me, or writing anything down, or recording anything I was saying on a small digital recorder she might have been holding in the palm of her hand. She had put her notebook back in her pocket, and her arms dangled at her sides. She looked past me. She looked over my right shoulder out into the habitat. I turned around. Andy swung on a vine. He swung on a vine with his Fittest Stick which I recognized from yesterday. He disturbed the habitat by jumping into it. He looked at us out of the corner of his eye and sidled over to the cooler.

"This is the journalist," I said to him. To the journalist, I said, "This is Andy, my intern." Andy froze.

"Where did you come from?" asked the journalist.

"I live up the road, in a clearing," Andy said, swinging his arms mechanically. "My father has a farm."

"I thought there were no more farms," said the journalist.

"There's only one left," said Andy.

"Holy Mackerel, what a story!" said the journalist. Andy came closer, regarded the journalist through his fogged spectacles.

"Has she told you about how the turtle laughs?" asked Andy.

"The turtle doesn't laugh," I said.

"How does it laugh?" the journalist asked.

"It laughs by chuffing. I made an experiment," said Andy.

I remembered the Copes-Brinkley cow with the unfamiliar tag upon her and I swear I choked.

"Andy, did you tag a Copes-Brinkley cow out of turn? Did you tag her for laughing?" I asked.

He had long wanted to make an experiment but I told him absolutely not because at that point we were here to monitor. This was a nice way of telling him that the Copes-Brinkley were not laughing, and what he took for laughing was probably just some stress response, a way of expressing fear of the feral pig.

"You think I haven't learned anything watching you out here every day all this summer, huh?" Andy said. "You think you can still just treat me like a sandwich maker even though I'm coming up to scientist status myself?"

"How does it laugh by chuffing?" asked the journalist.

"In the experiment, you can only hear the chuffing as a series of high frequency beeps. Not everyone thinks it's funny," he told the journalist.

"Oh, Andy," she said. She laughed. "How did you get the turtles to chuff?"

"I tickled them with a stick," said Andy.

"You've been poking the species with a stick?" I saw red.

"First time, I did it by accident to get our pig away, then the Cokes-Binkey started laugh-chuffing so I kept it up because I can tell it likes it," he said.

"There was a pig in the habitat and you didn't report it to me?" I asked.

"You were at the lab. I live here all the time," Andy said.

"This is bad," I said. "This is bad for the Copes-Brinkley habitat. One thing that's killing them is the feral pig."

"Our pigs aren't feral," said Andy. "If they were feral, they wouldn't be our pigs, they'd be their own pigs."

"Your pigs aren't feral?" asked the journalist.

"Well, they're semi-feral," said Andy. "But we can usually catch them when it's time for butchering."

"Fascinating," said the journalist.

"There's one back in those woods there," he said.

"Where?" I asked.

"Back in that briar," Andy pointed.

"See, that's what I mean, that's the habitat," I said, sweltering. Andy shrugged. The pig was rooting back there, in the mess of blackberry and alder, screened by thorns.

"Look, I'm only trying to save this one patch of habitat. For the Copes-Brinkley," I said.

"But who cares about them?" asked the journalist. "And I mean that literally. Literally, who? I'm certain many people do, and who are those people?"

"Me, for one," I said.

"But you're saying the turtle doesn't laugh?" the journalist asked.

"It's a turtle," I said. "It brummates. It breathes through its tail. Isn't that enough?"

"But you admit that it chuffs," she said.

"It chuffs, but so what?" I said, "This isn't some kind of coming-of-age story, Andy. This isn't your journey of personal discovery. The turtle doesn't laugh. And even if it does laugh, it doesn't matter that it laughs."

The journalist and Andy just looked at me and didn't say anything. They looked at me like two birds looking, like deer, like the woods watching, just watching. In the grove, the pig snuffled, sounding like a passel.

"I'm going to get that pig out of the habitat," I said. I went to the car. I opened the trunk, and took out the Winchester. The man at the pawn shop had thrown in extra buckshot cheap since I was a novice, and it was break-action and I put in five shells, and I turned back towards the beach ditch. Andy and the journalist still stood there, blinking at me.

And still, still! The deer were maddeningly wild!

"So you see where this has brought me?" I said. "I identify with the Copes-Brinkley. I take up its battles. I kill for it. And it crawls right by me like it can't see me."

I raised my shotgun, and Andy and the journalist watched me like a couple of damned twins. But a damp track of tamped down clay curved into the dark turn in the road where the willows bent over it. It was an outlet, and as I aimed out towards the thicket, a woman came out of the dark turn the track made. A ragged quick woman with a man's felt hunting cap pulled down over her ears.

"Wait!" she said. "Just what do you think you're aiming at?"

"There's a wild pig back in that briar." I said, already losing my resolve.

"Yes there is," she said. "Our pig. It's not even ready for butchering yet. You just put that gun down." I put it down.

"Who's that?" asked the journalist.

"You must be Andy's mother," I said. "Andy, my intern."

"Andy's who I've got," she said. She wore a complicated coverall, and beneath it, layers of wool and silk. She was weathered as everything else. "He's a solemn one. Always with his eyes brimming over."

"Mom," said Andy.

The journalist was rapt.

"I'm just trying to protect the Copes-Brinkley," I said. "The situation is dire."

"Me, I don't like the mud turtle much," the farmer's wife said, "always tunneling in my garden. But then, I suppose they deserve to live. What I mean is, maybe I'll kill them one by one, as pests, but I'm not a toxic environment, I'm not development, I'm not environmental devastation. I'm just one woman."

"I'm just one woman too. I'm a scientist," I said.

"I'm a journalist," offered the journalist.

"Ha. And I'm the farmer's wife," she said and spit beside her muck boots.

"Mom," said Andy.

"What? Don't be squeamish, Andy," said the farmer's wife. "I'd better get back," she said. "It's time for the old man's supper."

"Your husband?" asked the journalist, peeking out from behind me.

"I've heard of worse men, but I haven't met them in person," said the farmer's wife, spitting again thoughtfully.

"Your husband is a tyrant, then?" asked the journalist.

"He's exacting, is what he is," said the farmer's wife. "Any little thing. What we're talking about is a man who's content to live in filth, a black paste made of tar, coal, and grease. He's surrounded by it, but if anyone else so much as sets a spoon covered in maple syrup out of place, he begins to twitch. You see it in his jaw first. I'd better get back. You two come up and see us sometime. We're just up that hill, in the south clearing." She made to leave, then said, "Don't shoot what's not yours to shoot. What's in that gun, anyway?"

"Buckshot," I said.

"See there, you'd likely ruin it for any kind of eating. Andy, come on home now."

"Andy's been a great help to me," I said.

"That may be. But right now he's got gravel shoveling." She turned, her muck boots sucking back in the road, and she plowed her way back around the dark curve. Andy followed, taking his Fittest Stick with him. The journalist and I were left alone.

I offered her a soda pop, grape. I offered to show her the youngest Copes-Brinkley cow.

But she scanned the road in silence.

—

The journalist was not at the beach ditch the next day when I arrived at the habitat, though her car was parked in the same place. Andy also did not show. I did not see either of them all morning. I saw bubbles in the mud, spouts signifying eggs. I monitored them, but the spouts were oily. I saw the hump of an egg. It was speckled, marbleized. It did not have the waxen sheen of a healthy egg. A menacing mother moved. A Copes-Brinkley cow. She crawled from the black muck glaring. She made that spitting hiss common to all mothers in distress. I backed off, grasping for my oilskin notebook, my wax pencil. I scanned for the journalist. She should be getting this down. But she was not anywhere nearby. It was just the mossy primeval stuff, the vines.

Then the glen rustled, and a stinging smell came at me and a pig pushed through the thorns into the habitat. It took me in, swaying. Its back bristled. Its skin was pink and the hair covering it was long and black like the hair that surfaced in our sandwiches. Its eyes were still and shiny. Its tusks were filthy, layered with offal. I leapt up, and the pig charged me. I flailed. The pig lowered its head, came through the habitat. Tunnels collapsed beneath its turbine hooves.

Behind it, Andy burst through the thicket with a long stick, a fitter stick even than the one he'd had yesterday. Andy stopped when he came through the branches. He stopped and looked around. He saw he was in the habitat. Leaves littered his hair. His glasses were cocked to one side. He straightened them, he saw the pig, and he brandished his stick.

"Andy," I said. He must have seen me. The pig had me in its crosshairs, and I was the only person there. But Andy did not look at me. He kept his gaze riveted on the pig. It clambered up the bank, still making for me. I stumbled back, but at the last moment, it swerved to caper up along the track, around the curve of the road, up towards the clearing. Andy moved past me without speaking to me. He went after the pig, waving the stick. He made a noise with his tongue and his throat that the pig responded to. He followed the pig up the dark track. I followed him.

Around the curve the farm began, a mown clear hillside, with harsh hot wind, an ineffectual fence, some hollow stumps rolling around, chicken wire, rebar, scraps of
tin roofing sticky with tar. I passed a pogo stick sunk in
the mud, I passed the seat of a tractor rusting on its side,
a stack of broken windows, a beehive, a cat with no tail
stalked a heap of molding straw, a shed door banged and
banged again, blown open and shut by the wind. I cut my
calf on rebar. It went straight through my kevlar trousers,
and I could feel the sticky blood run down. I followed
Andy. I did not call for him again. Far up the hill, he drove
the pig into its hut.

Nearby, a rough pole shack listed into the muck. Smoke
came out of its chimney, though even at this hour of the
morning it was hot enough for me to wipe my brow with
my windbreaker. The shack was tall and narrow, with a
window high up near the pitch of the roof, though inch
for inch, the whole structure could not have been any bigger than my fried chicken stand. The farmer's wife came
slamming out its front door, swinging a plastic bucket.
She kicked the door closed behind her, went to the water
pump, and hefted the handle. Then she saw me.

"Hey, you scientist. You decided to come. Look at this
life, would you? I never wanted this," she said.

"Is the journalist up here?" I asked.

"Your friend with the big hair, marked like a skunk?
Ha."

"Is she here?"

"She's here alright," she said. "She wanted to ask me a whole slew of questions, mostly about the old man, that bastard. I guess it's good to tell my side of things for once. I told her to have a look around the place, but she mostly wants to eavesdrop. If I were you, I'd check behind the house there. I'll be with you shortly." Her bucket full, she rammed the pump handle back into place, then hauled the bucket into the shack again. Above, Andy shoveled gravel, his back carefully towards me.

So I stuck my head around the corner of the shack, and the journalist was there, crouching on the woodpile. She waved me towards her. "Get back here," she said, "if you want the scoop." So I got back there.

"Oh, boy," she said, flushed. "Oh baby, oh baby, holy mackerel. The way these people live. The stuff this farmer guy says to his wife. You wouldn't believe me if I told you."

"So just tell me," I said.

"Just listen," she said. She pressed her ear to the wall.

"The farmer's wife knows you're back here eavesdropping," I said.

"Of course she does," she said. "She wants me to get the whole story. We're crafting it."

I wanted back with my animal, but the farmer's wife came around the side of the house with some lemonade.

"It's hot out here," said the rosy cheeked journalist. She had become hearty. The farmer's wife's skin made wheeled pouches beneath her eyes.

"First she wouldn't even talk to me," said the journalist, "Now she's bringing me lemonade."

"I don't want you to get sunstroke following me around," said the farmer's wife. "Might as well give you some refreshment. We can spare it."

I finished my lemonade in one long draught. Felt my stomach go sour. Shifted. Wished to go. "Shall we go back to the site?" I asked the journalist. But she was sipping, eyes closed. She touched her tape recorder.

"I got a lot. Is that okay?" she asked the farmer's wife.

"Oh, lord," said the farmer's wife, but she looked pleased.

"She's at war with her husband," the journalist told me. "It's unbelievable, the stuff they say to each other. The farmer's wife is appalled that this is what her life has become. Do you know that she's traveled all over? She invented, you know, that thing. That thing. You know. You use it all the time."

"What thing?" I asked.

"Don't be absurd. That clip you use to keep the toothpaste tube rolled up so that it doesn't squeeze out all sloppy," she said. I looked at the farmer's wife.

"Oh, go on," she said. "It was hardly anything when it started. I didn't know it would take off like it did. Now I don't have time for inventions. Would you believe I used to compose music? Do you know what I hate most?"

"What?" asked the journalist. "Wait, while I turn on my recorder."

"I abhor a man who is quick to anger, then switches to a funny voice in order to draw attention away from his irritability," said the farmer's wife.

A man's voice from inside the shack called, "This is how you cook a squash? Do you think we're rich?"

"That's him," whispered the journalist, fumbling her recorder up against the battens. "That's the farmer. He doesn't know we're here."

"I'd better get back," said the farmer's wife, wincing. "Oh, he's very good today. He's in top form. Just keep your microphone to the wall." She took the empty lemonade glasses and went back around the side of the shack. We heard the door open and close as she went inside. The journalist motioned me to press beside her against the wall.

"Can you hear them?" she asked. "The farmer and his wife?" So I pushed close and I listened.

"They have these suicide nets," I could hear the farmer's wife saying inside the shack. "They string them up around certain factories to keep the workers from killing themselves. I heard it on the radio."

"Did you hear what the weather will be tonight?" The man's voice again, the farmer.

"You're not paying attention. I'm trying to tell you something interesting. Ever since they put the nets up," his wife continued, "the people jump into them. They jump out the windows, and then they're caught by the nets, but they die anyway. The nets don't stop them from dying. The nets are full of bodies. While up above, the workers keep working."

A sound like the slamming of a fist on a counter, then the farmer, "Windchill? Don't give me that. Unless you're going to be standing out in the direct wind with no cover. But who does that? It's misleading."

"Are you even listening to me? I am trying to tell you something edifying."

"And I'm trying to hear the weather report, but all they give me are lies about windchill."

"Windchill is not my fault, so don't take it out on me," she said. "And anyway, it's August."

"Did I say that windchill was your fault?"

"At any rate, they say it's going to be cold tonight," she ventured.

"I didn't say," he said deliberately, and I could hear his teeth gritting, "that it wasn't going to be cold."

"Is this about the suicide nets?" she asked. "Would you rather I didn't talk about them?"

"That's crazy. Why would it be about the suicide nets? I wasn't even listening to that. I was thinking about other things."

"Ignoring me, as usual."

I put my mouth next to the journalist's ear. She tried to bat me away, signaled that the farmer and his wife were still talking, but I said, "I don't have time for this."

"They've been married thirty years," she said. "They're the last family living in this godforsaken region. My God, They're so isolated they speak in a kind of resigned short-hand. Their stubbornness has become a pathology. They don't even smell the smell anymore."

"What are you saying?"

"Be inquisitive. Isn't that the first thing you learn in scientist school?"

"Is that supposed to be cute?" I asked.

"Okay, fine, what was the first thing you learned in scientist school, then? What? Something about peer review?" asked the journalist.

"What about peer review?" I asked.

"Yeah, what about it?" she asked.

"This isn't about that," I said.

"Then what's it about?" she asked.

We heard the shack door open and Andy's mother called for him. We heard Andy thump down the path. "Your father wants a word with you," said his mother. "You know how he gets when he's been up on the ridge for a few days. He wants to impart." The two of them laughed drily for a moment. Then the door closed. In a moment, the farmer's wife rejoined us behind the shack.

"I almost bought Andy a union suit for Christmas this year, but I froze up," she said, wringing her hands.

"That can happen with mothers and sons," said the journalist, to soothe her.

"Let's listen," said the farmer's wife. We all leaned in again. We could hear a chair being scraped back and a body creaking down into it. Then, heavy-footed pacing.

"Listen to me, Andy," came the farmer's voice.

"I'm listening." Andy was sullen.

"People say the young have no attention spans," the farmer said. "But what does this mean? The people who say so don't know that the attention span was invented by—"

Andy cut in, "By a gnat, a mosquito, a wasp-like waist, can I go?"

"Don't interrupt me, Andy. This isn't a joke. The attention span wasn't invented until 1930. By then, they already had shell shock. They already had the love affair with the automobile. Andy, are you listening? Stop doing that with your glasses."

The farmer's wife rolled her eyes at us. "This is from a man who storms out of the house when he loses a game. I beat him at backgammon this winter in the middle of a blizzard. He didn't care. He slammed out into the snowstorm. 'Marco,' we called. Nothing. And we didn't see him for two days. I thought he'd frozen to death and good riddance was my main feeling, despite him being a good provider, and stubborn. Then Andy came upon him huddled in a brush hut of his own making up along the ridge line. He would take no nourishment. He swore he didn't feel the cold. To this day, he says I play dirty. But listen to him in there. Confusing our boy. Andy's gentle, stalwart. He doesn't need a man like that to teach him history."

"We're on your side," said the journalist.

"I should hope so," said the farmer's wife. "What other side is there?" Then she was gone again. We heard the shack door slam.

"There's another tunnel network we might visit, if you want to get a sighting of the animal today. It's just down the track, back in the habitat," I said.

"We'd have to get down into the ditch?" asked the journalist.

"Yes, into the ditch. That's where they live. The ditches of beaches."

"Into the mire?" asked the journalist, looking at her red boots.

"Into the mire."

When she hesitated, I lost patience. "This story is about the Copes-Brinkley Mud Turtle, not about some farmer's wife," I told her. "You said it would be a series. I thought I could be a panelist."

The journalist looked at me with the same face she'd shown in the habitat the day before, when I'd aimed my gun into the thicket. It was a face of pure, bald observation, a face of incredulous and cool assessment. I could hardly stand it.

"Journalists and scientists aren't supposed to choose a thesis that sounds appealing and then just stick to it," she said. "That's the opposite of what they're supposed to do. In this profession, stories sometimes surprise us. We have a responsibility to follow them and see where they go." She waited to see what I would say, and when I said nothing, she sighed and leaned back against the woodpile. "I'm hungry," she said. "I wonder when Andy's going to be done talking with his father. I asked him to make us some sandwiches."

And so I came to monitoring the farmer's wife and her man, the farmer. I monitored them on the day that I should have been following the Copes-Brinkley into their final tunnel. On that day, I was instead far away. I was up the hill. I was in the south clearing. The journalist asked me to hold a microphone up to the wall of the shack, and I held it for her. I was assisting the journalist as I had never assisted anyone. I told myself it was because I hoped to lure her back. And when her story aired, "Who Cares about the Copes-Brinkley?" she mentioned the hog farms. She mentioned the stench. She mentioned the brummating, and the breathing through tales. And then, reedy and whistling, the farmer's wife's voice cut in.

"I'm not from here," she said, and in the background, you could hear the wind on that clear hillside, the shed door banging behind her.

"Where are you from?" the journalist's voice.

"Once," the farmer's wife said, "I rode a train cross country and an old lady said I had an aristocratic face. That means ugly and unhealthy, but I didn't care. Around here no one notices, but I lived for the ballet. I took a job fixing ice skates for the Ice Capades. I went to school. Wore slacks. A big brass safety pin held my coat together. I was rakish. I liked the glitz and glamour. Anything with sequins. Once, I made an outfit that was all silver and white feathers. I even had a headdress. I put it on, and I went out onto the ice, and I began to spin. All around me were everyday people just trying to have a garden-variety good time. No Hans Brinker. No The Red Shoes. No Sugar Plum Fairy. No. They wore tweeds and sweatshirts. They bundled in flannel. Of course, I didn't realize they were there at first. No. I thought I was alone. I flung my arms wide and began a complicated choreography of my own design. When I opened my eyes, there they all were.

All the other skaters. They had joined hands and were imitating me, in a long spiral, every workaday dad, and every latchkey kid, every amateur, every cousin and neighbor, they all spiraled out around the rink, and they did exactly what I did, step for step. And do you know why they did that?" asked the farmer's wife, her voice dropping to a throaty whisper. "It's because all of those people could tell that I was the one in charge."

—

On the day that the journalist's story aired, I packed my final crate out of the fried chicken stand. Much of my equipment had gone unused. I knew that the last of the brood had succumbed. I knew it was no use. I did not go back to be of use. But I went back all the same. I got in my lemon, and I drove out to the beach ditch. I parked under the sycamore. I opened the trunk, drew back the canvas tarp, and took up my Winchester. Carrying my gun, I stepped out into the cavern of empty muck. It was nearly October, though any scent of that was layered over by the familiar hundreds of chemicals. The Copes Brinkley would not brummate again. No turtle mother hissed. No mother encountered me. Andy was not there.

But one final time, just as I had hoped, I encountered the feral pig. I heard its busy rustling, its heavy hooves back in the thicket. It pushed through the briar as if called, and we regarded each other from either end of the Copes-Brinkley crypt. It raised its upper lip at me, and I could see its mossy fangs. It sent forth its smell of tang and sour rot. I lifted my gun into the crook of my arm. I raised my barrel to my shoulder. I sighted the pig, and I took my shot. The kickback punched me in the shoulder, and the sharp crack startled a pheasant, and startled me, and set the pig to rearing back, afraid, but still, the feral pig did not go down. My heart beat into the silence left by the sound of the gunshot. This was beyond me.

We all have names, alright? We all do. But sometimes we just want to be known by our professions. You think you're the only one? I was called Margaret. I was called Louise. I was called Alma. But we gave up those names when we took on our vocations. When you open the pages of an oversized book, one with lush painted plates, saturated with color reaching right up to each corner, this book is not full of first names. Rather, it is full of possibilities for the profession that can envelope you. The towns in this book are busy, are peopled by bakers, blacksmiths, carpenters, newsmen, bankers, tramps. Let us sink into these identities. Let us agree on titles that describe our true nature.

Oyster mushrooms clustered along aspen logs, gone too moist and wormy to be eaten. Blackberry and wood nettle rushed in to overtake the old tunnels. A black snake twined slowly through the drifts of red oak leaves, looking for a coil of other snakes to join in months of sleep. The pig burrowed away in a crosswise direction, and I could hear it rooting and snorting through the offal, and if it would soon be time for butchering, I didn't know anything about that.

What I mean to say is that all around me the forest continued to drip and sweat, to riot up and wither down by turn. The change I affected was unknown to me, and has remained wild and dark. Further than that, I cannot say, except that I met with no interruption.

THE PRIVATE FIGHT

*"Rulfo had an uncle who told him stories and when
Rulfo was asked why he didn't write anymore, his answer
was that his uncle had died."*

—ROBERTO BOLAÑO

Helen Conley loves a man who she caught recently
with his jaw slack and a book open in front of
him. He snapped both jaw and book shut when he saw
Helen coming up the path, but she knew for a fact that
the book reads America is the most exciting thing to have
happened to anyone in four hundred years. Nevertheless,
Helen Conley asked what the book was about, and he
said, Nothing, on September 11th of all days. How insen-
sitive. Talk about a case of the chickens coming home to
roost. So he said, Overpopulation. So Helen and her man
had an enormous fight, what's called knock down drag
out. First it was overpopulation, which he said is a big

problem, which she said is a fake big problem. So he said, Everyone agrees it is a big problem, and she what's called flew off the handle.

Just imagine someone you love being the ambassador of everyone, and delivering such an important message to you, the message that everyone agrees. Helen stopped thinking about overpopulation. She was overcome with jealousy. Who are all of these people, these everyones? These everyones that he's been agreeing with? Without me? Where was I when everyone was agreeing? He accused her of hysteria. She accused him of misogyny. So that's how the fight went. Overpopulation, then jealousy, and then they moved on to mowing. He hadn't done it in so long that they couldn't even walk because the undergrowth was so thick, the young vine maple, and the coltsfoot and the sword fern. You couldn't get back into the land. Your face would press right away against a wet plant, and the blackberry brambles would catch your cap off, and the huckleberries would dye you.

"We have to get back there!" Helen Conley yelled.

"Why?" he yelled back.

"Because it's our land!" she yelled. "We have to survey it!"

"It's not our land. That's a colonizer's perspective!" he yelled.

"Okay, but we are stewards of it and we have to traverse it!" she yelled. "And also the outhouse is back there. We have to get to the outhouse!"

He was pissed. He wanted to read his America is exciting book, which described how if people traveled through time on a ship from the 1600s, they would land in America and be astounded at the glory of it, while all the rest of the world would seem to them to just be ho-hum. These time travelers were Dutch, that's what the author was saying, and the rest of the world to them would basically be the same as they had left it in the 1600s: suspicious Japan, bossy China, beleaguered Europe, meaninglessly expanding Russia. But the United States—so populated, so engaging, wow! The author was a professor at Princeton University, but Helen Conley didn't care.

She told her man he had to mow. She took a breath and said, "You can't just sit on the couch all day reading an objectionable book while the forest starts creeping in and pressing against our faces unpleasantly." Then, because he refused to respond, she yelled, "I know for a fact that you don't like it when a wet plant presses against your face because you told me that yourself!" So her man threw the exciting book into the woods.

"What good does that do?" asked Helen.

"It expresses my true nature," he said, and then the phone rang. It was her uncle, Maxwell Conley in Seattle, who had raised her. "It turns out I'm sick," he said.

"Wait, wait," she said. Her man stalked up the path. She heard him turn up the top forty hits.

"I knew I was sick," her uncle Maxwell said.

"Wait, wait, hold on," said Helen. She sat down on a cinder block.

"I knew and I didn't know," said Maxwell Conley. "Your aunt says she knew. I just wasn't ready to find out until this week. Then I got ready. Now there's nothing they can tell me except that it's bad."

"Hold on," said Helen. "How bad do they say?"

"They don't know anything. It's not that they don't try, but it turns out that they just don't know," said Maxwell Conley.

"Wait, wait," said Helen, and didn't say, You are indispensable to me. Not just the fact that you observed me ad nauseum as a baby, and drew monstrous caricatures of my wide mouthed bawling. Not only that all my life you painted pictures for me on backgrounds of stubborn indigo. Catholic icons or a woodpecker in the same stroke, the Virgin springing from a teacup, a shock of daffodils. Not only for these reasons but for a reason even more selfish: Your entire unfathomable brain. I've used you as a library. I've used you as an excuse to be lazy. There is so much I haven't learned because I knew I could ask you. "Just hold on," said Helen, trying to think it all through. "I've got some questions. Before anything more happens, I'd like to take notes on this, so could you just wait until I get a pen." But of course she could not find a pen.

"I'll come home right away," she said. She had moved some way out of the city to try farming, the only pursuit that is sure.

"That's what I thought you would say," said Maxwell Conley, resigned.

Helen Conley found her man hacksawing the leg off a bed frame. "Turn down the music," she told him. She told him she couldn't find a pen. She told him the rest of what she knew. Considering it, they made up. She would go into the city. He would stay home and mow.

Helen's man began to load the truck for her and she stood in the gravel trying not to hate him. Yet her mind turned on the stultifying thought that she would only be able to love someone who knew her uncle as well as she did. The foregone defeat of this made her grind her teeth. No way to problem solve it. Nothing useful. Maxwell had been trouble, Helen Conley knew. Alcohol kept him up instead of putting him to sleep. Fueled on it, he battled her aunt Kay Svenson until he punctured her thigh with a ballpoint pen. This happened years ago. Before her own father left. Before Helen Conley was even three. Sober decades ensued, in which Maxwell expected the women in his life to dote on him and leave him alone in equal measure, and of course to read his mind. "Tell me I'm difficult. I know I'm difficult," he challenged them. But still, thought Helen Conley, he is how I understand myself.

"Why do you need a pen so bad?" asked her man.

"To write it all down," said Helen Conley. "To keep track of what I know."

———

Helen Conley knew this story: When Maxwell Conley was sixteen and in high school, with a bad attitude like many of us have, two young members of the Black Panther Party saved his life. It happened because a recent veteran of the war in Vietnam woke up one morning believing he was still in the jungle. Adrenaline began pumping through his body at impressive levels. He didn't have a gun, but he found an oak baseball bat in the alley behind his mother's apartment building. He laced up his combat boots. He stormed down the street until he came to the high school. He kicked open the doors of the school, and came through the hallway breathing hard, fists clenched around the bat. It was seventh period. The hallway was quiet. Around the corner came Maxwell Conley, cutting class as was his custom. He was not sober. He was wondering why Kay Svenson wouldn't pay attention to him in art class. He was admiring his long curly hair in the fleeting reflection of the fire extinguisher case mounted on the wall. His Converse sneakers flapped open and his unwashed socks came through. The Vietnam veteran, only a few years older than Maxwell Conley, met him in the hallway, and wasted no time. He drew back his boot and kicked Maxwell Conley to the ground, sweating. Each muscle in his neck stood out. He was scared and Maxwell Conley was scared. The veteran was black and Maxwell Conley was white. They never knew it, but they were both Catholic. Maxwell Conley would not be drafted as this young man had been drafted. Neither would Maxwell go to college. He would stay up all night and paint pictures of skeletons engaged in a dance of death. He would marry Kay Svenson. He would puncture her thigh. He would finally get sober after spending many nights in the bathtub. He would raise his brother's daughter, Helen. He would learn another language. Forty years later, he would get sick and learn what the doctors knew: not much. The veteran stood over him and brandished the baseball bat.

Maxwell Conley believed he would die. Red and yellow crept into the soldier's eyes. The soldier breathed fast through his nose, in Vietnam. Then the rapid sound of Beatle boots tapping down the hallway, and Murray and Phil Rose arrived. They were boys near Maxwell's age, brothers wearing powder blue shirts and black berets. Murray put his arms around the veteran, and Phil put his hands gently on the oak bat. Murray began to breathe with the young man and when their breathing matched, he slowed it down, and the man relaxed his hands, and Phil took the bat from him. Murray murmured to the veteran. "It's alright man," he said. "You're alright."

"You're alright," repeated Phil, until the soldier put his head down and began to shake. His knees gave way, and Murray hoisted him up, and then, supporting the man on either side, Murray and Phil Rose walked him down the hall and out of the building. The heavy door admitted daylight, then swung shut against it. Maxwell Conley was left alone, disregarded, lying on his back looking up at the ceiling tiles.

Later, sober, he saw Murray and Phil Rose smoking cigarettes out on the baseball diamond. They looked sharp. They were busy. They had a ten-point plan. Those young men wanted everything that had been promised to them.

Every acre, terrifyingly. Terrifyingly, they fed free breakfast to children and made a newspaper together and handed it out in the high school cafeteria. Maxwell Conley had no plan. He cut class and grew his hair long and smoked grass and wanted Kay Svenson to talk to him. He had been bussed in to the high school when the city finally had to do something about integration. He walked across the baseball diamond, kicking up red dust, to where Murray and Phil Rose sat on the bleachers, their stack of newspapers beside them. Murray raised his eyebrows, glanced at his brother.

"Thank you," Maxwell Conley said, "for showing up the other day. If it hadn't been for the two of you."

Phil looked at the sky. Murray looked at the ground. Phil said, "It was nothing, man."

"No, I mean it," said Maxwell, "I don't know where you guys came from. Out of nowhere."

Murray stubbed his cigarette out with one pointed boot. Phil scooped the stack of papers under one arm. They got to their feet.

"I mean thanks," said Maxwell.

"We don't take cream with our coffee," said Murray. Phil looked at Maxwell and shrugged. They left him standing there by the bleachers, one toe sticking out of his Converse, coated to his calves in red dust.

—

"That happened forty years ago," said Helen Conley's man, finished packing the truck. He had made sure she took a jar of tea, dented apples, a tow rope, her own bedding.

"What does that matter to me?" Helen Conley said. "It still isn't enough time. When you want to know someone, you'll just go on knowing them as long as you can, and when that knowing gets cut off, it will always be too soon."

"Have you ever been bored?" Helen's man asked her. "People worry about tedium. About teaming up."

"How can I be bored when there is so much to fight over and discuss?" she said, and she started up the truck.

—

When Helen Conley reached Seattle, her aunt Kay Svenson led her upstairs. "He won't get out of bed," she said. "This is new."

"What about you? How are you holding up?" asked Helen Conley.

"He's stopped painting," said Kay Svenson, pausing outside the bedroom door.

"I can fucking hear you," said Maxwell Conley from within.

"He's started carving," said Kay Svenson.

Maxwell Conley sat in bed carving the words WILL YOU MISS ME into linoleum, embedding them in repeating geometric patterns. He had lost a tremendous amount of weight. He was not even glad that Helen was there. Kay Svenson went to the kitchen and brought back mincemeat pie and cranberry sauce, though it wasn't a holiday.

"What a question," said Helen, picking up one of the prints.

"It's the old true song," said Maxwell Conley. "I knew you'd come but I didn't know you meant today."

"He wants to carve with no one watching," Kay Svenson told Helen.

"Leave me alone," said Maxwell Conley.

"Impossible," said Kay Svenson.

"I've been looking at you since we were sixteen," he said.

"Do I look the same to you as I did then?" she asked.

"Your lumps are lumpier," he said. "You still do the things that make me want to escape and stay. I'm hungry. Fuck this holiday food." So Kay Svenson took away the pie and went to go make him some tapioca.

"You tyrant, you really don't want us around?" asked Helen, when her aunt had gone.

"Why does she interrupt me?" asked Maxwell Conley.

"She loves you," said Helen. "She wants to help."

"She wants to be rid of me," said Maxwell Conley.

"What do you want?" asked Helen Conley.

"I want to be at the top of Mount Rainier where no one can bother me," said her uncle. He had a bag attached to him. "They're poisoning me to cure me and they can't even cure me. It's hell."

We rely on unanswerable and horrifying questions. Questions about hell and our souls and our own culpability and what if we were just a brain in a jar and how can we be so self-centered as to think that our existence is the axis on which all other existences turn, yet we cannot imagine our loved ones without us except that we are a fly on the wall. Maxwell Conley was more Catholic with each passing year, drawing comfort and terror from it, sticking out his tongue on Sundays so the wafer could be laid there. When Helen was a little girl, he had told her, It is lucky you're not Catholic though it is the one true religion. And small Helen Conley had asked, Why, and he had said, Here I am concerned with my soul, with one constant refrain from the time I was sixteen. But you don't have to worry about that and neither do I have to worry about you.

Helen had never taken notes on this. By Maxwell Conley's bed, she said, "When I was small, the thought of hell kept me up at night."

"Best laid plans," asked Maxwell Conley. "And now?"

"Now the thought of hell does not keep me up at night or concern me in the slightest," she said and fingered the linoleum block, WILL YOU MISS ME. She did not say, It is the simple fact of missing someone that will keep me up at night and I have been furnished with no strategy against it. She asked, "Are you really too sick to get out of bed?"

"White boy ain't go no soul," said Maxwell Conley.

"What?" asked Helen Conley.

"It's got me again. It won't leave me alone."

"What's that?" asked Helen Conley.

"You remember how the Black Panthers saved my life?" asked Maxwell.

"I just told my man that story," said Helen Conley.

"What did he have to say?" asked Maxwell.

"He said it happened forty years ago. To him that seems like a long time. What if I can't make him understand about time passing and not passing? About what makes some people feel like a dislocated joint?"

Maxwell Conley said, "Look at it this way. Your man comes from a culture of no pointing. If his people must make such a gesture, they do it with their thumbs or with their chins. When you accidentally point at him you can tell what has happened. The world doesn't exactly come to an end, but still, everyone feels bad."

"And so?" asked Helen Conley.

"So. Soon after Murray and Phil Rose left me on the baseball field, Martin Luther King Junior was shot and killed in Memphis, Tennessee. I went to school the next day. From a long way off, I could see a single figure standing at the school door, and as I got closer, I recognized Murray Rose. Murray stood guarding the door, motionless except for his cigarette. He moved it mechanically from his mouth back to his side. Other students drifted around the schoolyard in small, tense groups. Murray stood at the door, his face closed up, cold metal, and I was drawn there. I drew near to Murray, nearer, I came to the bottom step. Murray looked down, raised one powder blue arm, and pointed at me. It was as if he'd been waiting for me. He pointed at me and he said, 'White boy ain't got no soul.'"

"What did you do?" asked Helen Conley. She had never heard this.

"I dropped out of high school so that I would have more time to think about it," said Maxwell Conley. "I've been thinking about it ever since."

Maxwell told Helen how he had thought about white boy ain't got no soul throughout his life, when he was alone, when it was quiet, or when Helen Conley made a racket, or when Kay Svenson told him to get out of the bathtub, or when his brother didn't come home, or when he walked uphill, or when there was a strange animal, a bad time, a trip to the emergency room. Then he got sick. But that was nearly forty years later. Maxwell Conley would not be comforted.

———

Helen Conley stayed in the tiny guest room, only large enough to crawl into and go to sleep. She was kept awake at night be Kay Svenson and Maxwell Conley arguing, round and round, and she could not make out the words. She knew this: Maxwell Conley would not get out of bed. Soon he would not even take bland food, not even tapioca, but carved in bed all day darkly. He made himself unpleasant.

In the kitchen, Kay Svenson stood by the stove, a thoughtful hand to her chin. Helen Conley asked, "What should we do?"

"This is a tender time," said Kay Svenson, stirring. "It's maddening, but it's sweet."

"What do the two of you fight about?" asked Helen Conley.

"That would be hard to describe," said Kay Svenson. "He wants to know exactly where I am all the time and to get rid of me too," she said. "That's how it's always been. Don't you remember from when you were small?"

"He punctured your thigh."

"Do you remember that?" asked Kay Svenson.

"I wasn't yet three," said Helen. "But it's something you've both told me."

"I interrupted him too much, that was the trouble," said Kay Svenson.

Helen frowned. "If my man treated me that way, you'd tell me to leave him," she said.

"If I had ever stopped wanting to interrupt him, I guess I could have left," said Kay Svenson. "But I never stopped wanting to interrupt. There was a time when I ignored Maxwell Conley. I can hardly remember it, I'm so changed. I was fifteen. We had art class together. He tried to impress me with wild blue paintings, smoking dope in the back of the class, playing fiddle tunes. In those days, I could balance on all the highest walls, so that I hardly ever walked on the sidewalk like other people. I skated down railings, hopped up on fences. I wore a long ponytail and high red socks. Maxwell Conley was beneath my notice."

"What happened?" asked Helen.

"I noticed him. After that, I never stopped noticing him."

"Did he tell you why he won't get out of bed?" asked Helen.

Kay Svenson nodded. She said, "A few years ago now, I saw Murray Rose at the supermarket. He moved back to town, worked different jobs, he said, construction, taxi driver, then he went back to school. Works at our old high school now. Teaches history, I think. He married, had kids too, they must be around your age. So many of our generation stayed here. When I think I live less than a mile from where I was born. They say the modern world's not like that, but then here we are." She put a spoonful of tapioca into her mouth. "I don't like this much myself," she said and spit it into the sink. She put her arm around Helen Conley's waist. "How's that man of yours?" she asked.

"Same fight," said Helen Conley. "Not yours, that's not what I mean."

"No, of course not," said Kay Svenson. "Your own fight."

"Yes," said Helen Conley. "Over and over again."

———

Helen Conley found Murray Rose in front of the high school. School was just letting out. She heard a teenager call Murray's name, and she followed the answer. Murray leaned on the chain link fence, easy and happy, raising his hand as the busses pulled away. His hair had grey streaks and was held back with a rubber band. He waved at the high school kids with their bad attitudes, their yelling and cat calls, he gave them guff right back and knew all of their names. Helen Conley waited. He smiled at her, taking her for a younger parent maybe, someone with business in the school. She could see his gold eyeteeth. She introduced herself. She said, "I'm Maxwell Conley and Kay Svenson's niece."

"Sure, sure," he said. "I went to school with your aunt. This was our neighborhood," he added, "but they bussed your family in. I saw Kay a few years back. How's she doing?"

"My uncle Maxwell's sick," said Helen. Murray Rose kept a question on his face. "Maxwell Conley," said Helen.

"I'm sorry to hear that," said Murray Rose. "Must be hard on Kay."

"It is," said Helen, but this was not what was meant to happen here. She had to change it. These were her uncle's talismanic stories, these were how the generations would understand each other, even though each had to go forward alone. "My uncle Maxwell says you saved his life," she said.

Murray Rose raised his eyebrows, stayed polite. "Maxwell—what did you say his last name was?" he asked.

"Maxwell Conley. Conley. Same as my last name. He was always getting into trouble and the teachers wanted to throw him out. He wouldn't cut his hair. He played fiddle tunes in the halls. He did acid in math class when they talked about fractals," Helen Conley said, fighting her rising breath.

"Wild kid, huh?" said Murray. "Still a bunch of wild kids at this school. Some things don't change." He folded his arms, looked up the street.

"He says if you hadn't stood up for him, he would have been killed. You and your brother, Phil."

"Is that what he said? Well, maybe that's true. We can't know. Phil and me, when we saw something happening around here, we'd do something about it."

Helen Conley struggled to stay calm. She struggled to ask Murray about we don't take cream with our coffee and she found she could not do it. Yet if she was too shy to ask about that how would she ask about the other thing? How could she ask about white boy ain't got no soul? My generation has not been given the proper vocabulary, she thought. There was no ease. A time traveler arrived from the era when the sixteen-year-olds had been frank about race, had said what was on their minds even when it hurt people's feelings and made them uncomfortable, even when they made mistakes. It was high stakes. They were teenagers, and they demanded enormous changes, so someone had to say something. Or that is what Helen Conley wished would happen, but no time traveler arrived.

"There was a veteran," she told Murray, her face hot. "He had a flashback."

Murray looked back at her. "Oh yes," he said. "I remember that. That young veteran. Wallace Sever was his name. His mother still lives down the street from here. Phil and I, we didn't want him to do something he'd regret. He was eligible for VA benefits and didn't even know it. He went to the hospital after that. Back then, they didn't have a name for what was happening to the young men coming home. But you could see it in people in the neighborhood. Now you see it again."

"That was Maxwell Conley," said Helen. "The kid that Wallace Sever came after with a bat. That was my uncle Maxwell."

"Wish I had a better memory," said Murray Rose by way of apology. He straightened, put his hand out. "Good to meet you," he said. "I'm glad you young people want to learn about those times."

"Wait," said Helen Conley. "My uncle Maxwell would like to see you again."

"Me?" asked Murray Rose.

"He won't get out of bed," said Helen.

"He's that sick?" asked Murray.

"He just won't, that's all," said Helen. "He's been asking after you." Murray Rose folded his arms again. "Haven't seen the man since high school," he said. "Can't honestly say I'd know him if I saw him."

"It would mean a lot to my aunt Kay," said Helen Conley.

Murray Rose nodded. "Sure, I'll come over. I'll be happy to do that."

—

He brought a casserole, and Kay Svenson put it in the freezer and Maxwell Conley got out of bed. He came downstairs and sat on the sofa. Murray Rose sat near him. Neither of them were big men, but Maxwell Conley had begun to look like a cat mummy with the most beautiful eyes. The two men wore button-down corduroy shirts, tucked in. Murray's was red. Maxwell's was turquoise. Murray, though fit, had a belly that stuck out proudly over his belt. He wore soft leather shoes that some people might accuse of being slippers but were not slippers. Maxwell Conley wore slippers.

"Look at us, we both look like hippies all these years later," said Murray. "We lived through some wild times." If he still did not remember Maxwell Conley, he didn't say so.

"I got sober thirty years ago," said Maxwell.

"Is that right?"

"But now I smoke a little pot sometimes. It's because I'm sick."

"Helen told me and I'm sorry to hear it," said Murray.

"What about you? How's your health?" asked Maxwell.

"Gets more painful," said Murray.

"How's your brother?" Maxwell asked. "How's Phil?"

"Phil went to Canada. Hasn't come back yet. Our mother went up there too, a couple years ago, to be with the grandkids." Murray said. "Still see them on Christmas though. He was drafted, you know, right out of high school."

"I never heard that," said Maxwell Conley. "I never heard about that."

"Well, a lot of you white boys dropped out of school," said Murray. "Most of you were never around. But we were always around. We were trying to get things done."

"Do you feel that you got things done?" asked Maxwell.

"There's always more to do," said Murray.

"I don't know that I ever got anything done," said Maxwell. "I just wanted this woman to marry me." He held onto Kay's leg to steady himself. She stood by the sofa.

"Murray, I'm glad you came," Kay Svenson said. "This is the first time he's got out of bed in the last week."

Helen Conley could see that her uncle would not say what he wanted to say. When faced with it, he had the good sense to not ask an innocent man, a man he had not seen in forty years, a man who maybe didn't remember him, whether or not he had a soul. Yet he worked it around in his mind. It preyed on him. Courage, maybe foolishness, was called for.

Helen Conley asked, "Do you remember where you were when Martin Luther King Junior was shot?"

"I saw it on the evening news," said Kay Svenson. "Walter Cronkite did a special report."

"Sure," said Murray, "And isn't it strange to think that we all went to school the next day? No one thought we should stay home. But of course at that age, you want to be out in the world."

"My uncle always talks about that day," Helen said.

Maxwell Conley was silent.

"That was a hard day," said Murray. "A cold day. That was a long time ago."

They sat side by side on the sofa.

Murray gestured to the rosary beads on the mantle. "You still practicing?" he asked.

"Yes," said Maxwell. "You?"

"Lapsed," said Murray.

"The worst part about being sick is that I want to be alone but no one will let me," said Maxwell Conley. "Parts of my life come back to me: skateboarding down the hairpin turns, climbing a peak when a lightning storm rolled in so that all my hair stood up like a halo, being very small and waking up before my parents so that I could play with lead soldiers in the dark, waking in the bathtub at noon when the house was empty. The last time I did each of those things I didn't know it was the last time. Or that I would observe myself doing them from this place, with such bewildered longing. You said something to me those many years ago."

"I did?" asked Murray.

"Yes, and I wanted to ask you about it," said Maxwell.

"Better not to," said Murray.

"But sometimes I suspect you were right," said Maxwell. "I have thought about it many times."

"Better just to leave it be," said Murray Rose.

Kay Svenson brought some coffee.

When Helen Conley followed Murray out to his car, he said, "That's been keeping your uncle in bed, huh? One cold thing I said to him when we were teenagers?"

"You remember that then? Pointing at him?" asked Helen. "You remember what you told him?"

"I communicated so much back then," said Murray Rose. "I said what was on my mind. With age, I have become more diplomatic." He stepped off the curb, and walked around to the driver's side, opened the door, then stopped. He looked at the ground, and pursed his lips. He reached in to his car, took a pack of cigarettes from the dashboard, shook one out, lit it. "Do I need to say this?" he asked, looking at the sky. "When Dr. King was killed, I felt like what's the fucking point. Sure, we had already railed against pacifism. We had our own ideas about change coming. But then, that day, that bad day, I had no sympathy left for anyone, not for anyone white or black, and no way for someone like your uncle. I felt so low, I felt so mean. They almost shut down the school after that. We wanted to burn it down." He exhaled smoke through his nose. "It is a problem for white people," Murray Rose said. "And it will continue to be a problem. Benefitting from such soullessness over the years, I mean. But it's not my business to make sense of that. I couldn't do it even if I tried. And remember, I was a teenager, just like Maxwell. I was sixteen. And now I'm old and tired too, and I don't have the answers he wants. I didn't care if I hurt anyone's feelings then, and I don't want to hurt your uncle's feelings now, not when he's sick and worried, but if he wants to sit there turning us into symbols, it just won't work, man, and it'll only make things worse. You think I know more about souls than you people do? Do you think that's because I'm black? I don't think you get it. If you ask me, I'll tell you soul is a style of music. I'm no priest." He swung down into his car.

———

When she came back into the house, there was no satisfaction. Kay Svenson took up the coffee cups, put down pieces of pound cake. Maxwell Conley lay back on the sofa blinking upwards.

"Do you think you made a mistake?" asked Helen.

"I've got time to make mistakes," said Maxwell Conley. "It's one of the only things I have time for. I'll get what I deserve."

"It's good to see someone from so long ago," said Kay, sitting down next to him, putting her hand on the back of his neck just inside his shirt collar. "Only so many of those."

"Are you comforted?" asked Helen.

"There's no comfort," said Maxwell. "My soul is at the top of a mountain," he said. "No, it's down in the shadow of the mountain. Tucked down in the trees."

Helen Conley said, "I can't understand it. I can't understand what I am supposed to do about it."

"About what?" asked Maxwell Conley

"About missing you," said Helen Conley.

"I can't figure it out either," said Kay Svenson.

"It's your own fault," said Maxwell Conley. "I told you, Kay. Don't hitch up with someone you can't live without because chances are that you'll have to live without them someday, either by divorce or by death. So choose someone you are very fond of but not chemically dependent on."

"Cold comfort," said Kay Svenson.

"But what about me?" asked Helen Conley. They looked at her. "I never chose you," she said. "I did not hitch up with you. I was born to our relationship. I was not even aware of our bond forming. I was busy squalling and making mucus. It's not fair to scold me now for getting too attached to you and for missing you so that it stifles my breath." She had to stop talking.

Kay Svenson and Maxwell Conley did not answer her, but turned to each other. Helen Conley could see that they wanted to have their fight, their same fight, the private one. So she got in her truck and drove home.

—

This last time, when Helen Conley and her man fought, she began to cry, as ends most of the fights between those two, and Helen's man put his arms around her and breathed with her, and when their breathing matched, he brought her to the ground. And because they were already on their hands and knees, they began crawling through the woods. It was the only way they could get through, as he still had not mowed. Helen Conley followed her man through horsetail and hemlock saplings, through skunk cabbage and twinflower and stinging nettle. They crawled past the America is exciting book. Puffball mushrooms grew from it. They were down very low.

"See," he said. "You can still get through. You can still go walking in the woods."

"We're not walking," Helen said. "We're crawling."

"You're right," he said, which cheered her. "We can crawl through it. Do you see how things look from down here?" And he showed Helen plants she did not know, that grew down there, devils cub and bleeding heart, piggyback plant and false solomon's seal. He pulled wild ginger and they bit into it. Helen blew her nose and said, "If I have forty years to get to know you better, it would still not be enough time. I want to get to know you as long as they'll let me. Because my uncle discouraged Catholicism in me, I do not know who I mean by they, but I know that I'll take more time if they'll give me more time. So what if it's for our whole lives? Do you have something else you need to be doing?" Then she remembered that you can't command people to love you, so she said, "It's alright if you're too busy."

"I'm not busy," he said. He cried some too, but she thought he was just breathing in a funny way. They kept crawling through the woods until they met a buck that was knee-walking through the undergrowth. They watched it. It knew they were there but pretended not to know. It stayed low. Then Helen said to the buck, "This knee-walking plan you have is not a good one." Her man said to the buck, "You should get up and run. We are going to crawl out of here and get the gun, and if you're still here when we come back, we're going to shoot you and eat you for dinner." The buck looked at them with its blank deep eyes. It stretched its neck long and flicked one ear. It did not get up and run.

Helen Conley and her man crawled out of the woods. They got the gun and some rope and their sharp knives and some wax paper. They crawled back through the green tunnel they had made in the undergrowth, and the buck was still there. So Helen shot the buck, and they hung it from a vine maple, and they skinned it and gutted it, and they butchered it, and they wrapped the meat in packages, and they saved the stomach for blood sausage, and they kept the legs whole for salting and hanging, and they left the carcass beneath the maple for the coyotes. It took them the whole day.

———

Helen Conley's uncle, Maxwell Conley is still sick and what he wants most is to be unmanaged. He wants to be twelve years old and alone with his dog, coming down Mount Rainier in the night, down past the timberline, where the Douglas firs begin. He wants to come through the firs among the shafts of silver that make each thing darker, the path before him a running shadow, a gleaming stone, a vernal pool. He wants to be alone with his dog trying to make it back to camp by morning. He wants to be alone. But he is surrounded, and his great fear is that he won't ever be able to be alone again, and he knows that death itself doesn't count.

THE BIG WOMAN

Marcus called out level and chalk line and finishing hammer, nail gun, drywall, and joist hanger. He called out two-by-six, angle finder, button caps, stepladder, and spray foam. At twelve thirty he called out lunch and he sat in his truck to eat a bologna sandwich, and he suspected that his boss, Gordo, hated his own child. Marcus was working on Gordo's new house, designed to be a mansion if they could get the roof up before winter. Meanwhile, Gordo and his wife and child lived in the old house smashed right up against the new one. Gordo called it a shithole, swore to level it to the ground once his mansion was complete. It was pretty much already winter if they were honest but they didn't talk about it and worked by shop light until they couldn't feel their fingers. Shop light, Marcus called out each night into the cloud of his breath, LedgerLok, spider bit.

Gordo said he liked mountain biking but Marcus never saw him do it and it was difficult for Marcus to believe that Gordo had any kind of carefree hobby. Gordo was the only rich person that Marcus knew personally. He came from Los Angeles, where he had been a contractor to the stars. When Marcus ate his bologna sandwich, Gordo watched him, working his mouth, pretending not to watch. Marcus was back at work inside half an hour, calling out speed square.

They had met when Gordo dragged a trampoline out into the street and put a piece of cardboard on it that said "FREE." Driving past, Marcus thought that if he took the trampoline home, maybe someday he would have children.

"You got kids?" Marcus asked Gordo when he parked next to the trampoline.

"A son," said Gordo.

"Won't he miss this trampoline?" asked Marcus.

"He's not like other kids," said Gordo. He looked at the tools in the back of Marcus's truck. "You know anyone who needs work, let me know," he said. "I've got to get my new house up before winter or my wife will kill me."

"Who else have you got working for you?" asked Marcus.

"No one, goddammit," said Gordo. "In this town it's like maybe I'll work after I finish this beer and smoke this joint, well not on my dime. These guys don't seem to get it, I'm not from around here, I'm from out there, and I don't put up with that shit. My wife's got FBI clearance, she's a financial consultant. Unlike some people. I met an expert who showed me how to get the most from my employees."

"How?" asked Marcus.

"If you work for me, you call out the name of everything you do as you're doing it."

"Everything?" asked Marcus.

"Every tool, every task," said Gordo. "That way, not only do you know what you're doing, but I know what you're doing. You think if you had to call out everything you were doing on the job site, you'd call out 'finishing a six-pack'? Or 'scratching my ass'? Not likely. This expert, he was an expert in time motion. It's a method. It cuts down on unnecessary activity and I know I'm getting my money's worth."

Marcus had no wife, but a wife was what he wanted, and he knew that one day a big woman would walk out of the woods, out of the gathering darkness, and claim him. So he had bought a small piece of land and a goat. The goat was intended for milk. The land was five acres and still not paid off, and Marcus waited there for the big woman. He waited, sleeping in his trailer on the edge of his land, right up against the road. He kept the goat tied to a stake under a piece of roofing, and he was afraid of the dark. So Marcus agreed to help build Gordo's new house, though he could tell from the beginning it would be a trial.

———

Marcus took the trampoline home but the trampoline had a hole in it, and also, Marcus could think of nothing so foolish as a grown man jumping on a trampoline all alone. Slowly, Marcus was filling up his land with important materials. Each piece was to attract his wife, to show her that he was a man of means, of big plans, but sometimes he worried his wife might not really get it, might not understand why he needed two cargo carriers and an oversized drab net with a hole in it and a metal toolbox housing a persistent wasps' nest and a refrigerator turned on its side and a long cafeteria table, all left out in the weather. A wife might want to get rid of those things.

Nevertheless, Marcus brought the trampoline home, past all the predatory dogs. He was afraid of the dark, but he pretended not to be. He left the trampoline in the back of his truck and fed his goat, who stamped at him, reproaching him with yellow eyes. The goat was meant to forage, but he had not yet figured out a fence and did not want to let her off the stake while he was gone. Marcus shoveled some alfalfa to her. Quickly, he went back and forth to his woodpile, and he built his fire while it was still light out. He pissed, brushed his teeth, and spit the toothpaste into the bear grass, all this while it was light, and then, as the sun disappeared, he shut himself tightly into his trailer, and turned up the lantern. I had better build a house, thought Marcus. That is what a big woman would really want. But instead he sat in his trailer and looked out the window.

Through a sparse screen of blackberry bushes, he could see the thieves who lived across the road. Happily, they leaned on tire irons in their driveway, loosened lug nuts, revved engines, drank cloudy water from a milk jug, and threw pieces of plastic onto a large fire. They showed no regard for the sunset. As far as Marcus could see, they were all men, but Marcus knew they were a family because most of them had the same last name, and he knew that families usually included women, and he knew that when the thieves scoped people's property, they carried with them a mean little baby sucking on its fist, silent and bald with glittering eyes.

Marcus watched them now, and he saw the biggest one, the oldest one, the dad thief with the gray beard, mop his face with a large rag, and heave a tractor tire upright so he could roll it into the fire. Marcus could see a plastic doll with one missing leg in the creek. A young thief stood on the sandstone bank, throwing glass bottles at the doll. He held the baby over one shoulder. The doll sank. The baby threw his arms into the air. Everyone, it seemed, was busy except for Marcus.

—

At work, Marcus called out piss, and Gordo came around the house and said, "My wife saw you pissing in the bushes, and she asked me why aren't the locals house trained, so why don't you go inside our house if you need to use the bathroom. Just take your boots off. What kind of operation do you think I'm running?" Marcus didn't want to enter Gordo's house, but he saw no alternative, so he went around back and in through the screen door. The heat hit him in the face, thick, yeasty, demoralizing. The living room was in the basement. Batteries, diapers, and boxes of wet wipes loomed in the corners of the cramped rooms. Marcus could hear Gordo's son screaming up on the first floor, and beneath that, the ticking of a mechanical swing. The only light came from one small window above the sofa, and Marcus made out a large framed jigsaw puzzle on the wall. It was a photograph of Gordo and his infant son, sleeping together.

Shuddering, Marcus found the scummy bathroom. He pissed and washed his hands with vanilla-scented antibacterial soap. Back outside, he yelled extension cord and picked one up and plugged it in. He built a shitty wall. Marcus considered the jigsaw puzzle, and it was an outrage. A lie. Well, not a lie, but an outrageous omission. Here was an exact case, Marcus thought, of the exception proving the rule. Because everyone has to sleep sometime. So if you accuse someone of being an unrelenting fucking asshole and the only time when this is not true is when he's asleep, then you have been proven right.

—

Marcus didn't know that once, Gordo drove all night across three states to see a specialist and yet his small son cried and cried and continued to hold his body completely stiff. His cries took on a high-pitched bleating. A person could get impatient, the books said it was normal, how could Gordo teach a son like this to make money and not be taken advantage of in this world, to let people know who they were dealing with? Only when the boy slept would he let his limbs go limp, and the drool would spin out of him fine and steady as a spider's web. He didn't care about trampolines. He didn't care about wheels, cranes, or mulch piles. Angrily, Gordo wore his son's tiny winter hat because he could not find his own hat, and still he called his son "that little asshole."

—

The thieves cut into Rudy's toolbox and stole his thirty-six-inch chain-saw bar. The thieves walked right into the yurt of the mill operator and took her springform pan and two rounds of antibiotics. The thieves took the crossbow from the front room of Aldi Birch's place, just walked in, opened the coat closet, and took it. The thieves drove their pickup truck around and around on the front lawn of Seth Cordy, who would not allow them to swim in his pond. He ran outside shaking his fist, and the thieves drove right over his pear tree, crushing it. So again, there was a neighborhood-watch meeting.

Everyone knew who the thieves were, and the sheriff knew too. At the meeting, held at the yurt of the mill operator, the sheriff's deputy told people what they already knew, which was that the baby was how the thieves made themselves more appealing. The sheriff's deputy told the people what they had already experienced, which was that the thieves would come over with the baby and would offer to buy things from you or say they had lost their dog. The thieves liked to say, "I've walked these hills all my life," and gaze wistfully around. And though it was a pretense, it was also true. The people at the neighborhood-watch meeting agreed that it might be harder to be the thieves than it was to be the people that were being stolen from. Drugs and suddenly you're older and your dad, the head thief, is still telling you what to do, and you can't get any real respect. Rudy offered to patrol the road with his semiautomatic, which he felt would give the thieves an even chance. The sheriff's deputy sighed and drank the cup of coffee that was offered to him.

Marcus came back from the meeting and his goat was gone. The stake was pulled out of the ground. The rope had been cut through. Marcus looked across the road, at the thieves' compound. One strand of wood smoke trailed up from the chimney of the double-wide. Framed in the doorway, he saw the silhouette of one thief, the blooming tip of his cigarette. As Marcus watched, the man raised his hand and waved. Marcus waved back. The man rose. And then the crunch of gravel and the young thief crossed the road and stood before him, holding the baby, spitting at the ground, and squinting at Marcus. The sun had gone down, which Marcus didn't like.

"This is Bexley," the young man said, shoving the baby into Marcus's arms. The baby, a squirming damp bundle in a nappy hooded jumpsuit, farted loudly and began to hiccup. "He's my kid. Just like his dad, too, the little shit. I'm Dustin. You're Marcus. Learned it from the mailman." He took a bottle from the hip pocket of his coveralls, handed it to Marcus. "He's probably hungry," Dustin said. Marcus offered the bottle to Bexley, who clamped down immediately and sucked, his breathing coming in squeaking grunts. He kept his unfriendly gaze fixed on Marcus, who held him out slightly from his body, unsure. Marcus bounced him. Bexley screeched. Marcus stopped bouncing him.

"So you bought the place?" asked Dustin.

"That's right," said Marcus.

"You from around here? Haven't seen you," said Dustin.

"I'm from Washington County," said Marcus. "Came down here to find work. Found this piece of land."

"This place isn't really for living on. It's more of a hunting place," said Dustin.

"Well, I'm living here," said Marcus.

"I was thinking of buying that trampoline. Is it for sale?" asked Dustin.

"I was thinking of keeping it," said Marcus.

"You got kids?" asked Dustin.

"Not yet," said Marcus.

"Before you got here, I almost considered this place to be mine, for how much we were over here, growing up. No one ever lived here. We used it for hunting. My name is carved into more than one tree. Have you seen that?" asked Dustin.

"Not yet," said Marcus.

"What happened to your goat?" asked Dustin.

"It must have got loose," said Marcus.

"I haven't seen it," said Dustin. "But you shouldn't leave a goat tied up all day."

"That's true," said Marcus.

"One goat gets depressed, just like one person. Hate to see that. You should have at least two," said Dustin.

"You're probably right," said Marcus, and began to feel guilty.

"You hunt?" asked Dustin.

"Haven't got a gun," said Marcus, then thought to add, "But I've always wanted one."

"If I still wanted to hunt on this land, what would you say about that?" asked Dustin.

"I don't see any problem with that," said Marcus.

"We could go out together sometimes," said Dustin.

"Really?" said Marcus.

"Sure," said Dustin. Delicately, Bexley spit up down Marcus's arm. He did not change his cross-eyed glare.

"He only does that to people he likes," said Dustin, his face solemn. Then he grabbed Bexley and swung him up in the air. "Come on, Tiny," he said. He pitched his voice high, sang out, "Hoody hoo hoo! Goony goo goo!" He snuggled the baby down into the bib of his coveralls, against his flannel shirt. Bexley frowned and gave a dry cough.

"Come over sometime," said Dustin. "I've seen you looking over. Come over to the fire. Drink a beer, whatever."

"Okay," said Marcus. "Thanks."

"Sorry about your goat," said Dustin, "But like I said, you can't just keep a goat tied up outside like a dog. They're meant to forage."

"Yes. You're right. Thank you," said Marcus. Dustin pushed back through the blackberries and went across the road, with Bexley punching the air in front of him.

Marcus went into his trailer and pulled the blinds over the window that faced the road. He hoped the blackberry bushes would get bigger. He considered what Seth Cordy had told him at the meeting, that you don't want to get too friendly with those guys, but then you don't want to get on their bad side either. Look at what they done to me, said Seth Cordy. I'd see less of them if we were friends. Jiminy. If you care about your pear tree.

———

During the first snow, Marcus showed up to work and Gordo had a moving van parked at the dead end. He told Marcus they were going to pick up a planer, an upright band saw, and a table saw that he'd bought off a woman whose husband had stuffed her into a construction dumpster. "He thought she was dead but she wasn't dead," said Gordo. "He's in prison. It's a good business opportunity."

"Do we have to call out what we're doing while we're there?" asked Marcus.

"No," said Gordo. "It might freak her out, so just call it out on the inside."

When they got there, the woman was waiting in the snow with her two sons, all of them wearing earmuffs. She was beautiful and her sons were noisy and disturbed, dragging pieces of tarps and overpronouncing words. Snowball had six syllables the way they said it. Marcus hoped they had been asleep while their dad stuffed their mother into a dumpster but he worried that they'd been awake. The beautiful woman laughed breathlessly and had false teeth. This is what happens, thought Marcus. People lose their teeth. It happens to everyone. It's the thing that levels the playing field. This could be her, thought Marcus uncertainly, and threw snowballs at her children. One son hit the other son in the penis, and he fell to the ground, rolling in the snow. "It kills, it kills!" he cried.

"I hit you in the nads!" the other son yelled. Nads had three syllables the way he said it.

"Don't do that," Marcus told him.

"My dad's in jail," the son said.

"That's true," said the beautiful mother, overhearing. "I tell them it's okay to talk about it," she said. "We had a domestic-violence situation. It's okay to talk about it."

"It's okay to talk to me about it," said Marcus and was not sure if she heard him. How will I know? wondered Marcus. How will I know when my big woman arrives? Gordo tried to move the three-hundred-pound upright band saw by himself. "Fuck it," he said and he got a dolly. He got the moving van stuck in the snow. He told the sons to get the hell out of the way.

On the way home from work, Marcus stopped and picked up a six-pack. He parked behind his trailer and walked across the road. He found Dustin and another young man, leaning against a gleaming dirt bike, in the garage. Bexley kicked in a car seat near his dad's foot, sucking furiously on a pacifier.

"Marcus," said Dustin, "what's happening? I was just telling my cousin Clyde."

Marcus stuck out his hand, but Clyde just looked at it.

"He's from Washington County," said Dustin. "Thought he'd try his luck here."

"I brought some beers," said Marcus, holding out the six-pack. Clyde took one.

"Clyde's shy," said Dustin.

"Are we taking this thing out tonight or what?" asked Clyde, rapping the bike's fender with his knuckles.

"Fuck if I know," said Dustin.

"Where's Faith? She's coming over to watch Bexley, right?" asked Clyde.

"Fuck if I know," Dustin said. "Bexley's mom," he told Marcus. "We're still together and everything, but we had some trouble so she went off." Marcus nodded.

"You're not still together," said Clyde, "More like you wish you were."

"Fuck you, Clyde, don't spread my shit around the neighborhood. Can't even say hello to Marcus and shit, and then just open your mouth to say shit you don't know shit about."

"That's okay," said Marcus.

"Totally uncivilized," said Dustin. "But it's true, what he's saying, kind of. She's my true love. Are you married?"

"No," said Marcus. "But I wish I was."

"Technically I still am," said Dustin, "but we need to renew our vows or something."

"None of that for me, man, no thanks, too much trouble," said Clyde.

"Fuck you, man, it's heaven," said Dustin. He finished his beer, then took another from the six-pack. "Precious treasure. I'd do anything for her."

"Except live with her," said Clyde.

"Fuck you, Clyde, you don't know a thing about it," said Dustin.

"Too much strife," said Clyde. He used a plastic Kroger's card to separate a pile of chopped-up white powder, then leaned over the seat of the dirt bike and snorted it up his nose.

"It's not what you think," said Dustin, catching Marcus looking. "It's a painkiller. It's for his pain."

"Yeah," said Marcus.

"You work?" asked Dustin.

"In town," said Marcus. "For that new guy at the dead end."

"The guy from LA?" asked Dustin.

"Right," said Marcus.

"He's got a lot of stuff over there. Just lets it sit out. That must be how they do it in California," said Dustin. "Anyone told him his mansion is going to slide down the hill into the river?"

"I've told him that myself," said Marcus, "but he won't listen. Hey, if he wants to pay me."

"Right?" agreed Dustin. "I've done that kind of work before. Does he need more guys?"

"You never worked an honest day, who are you kidding?" said Clyde.

"Fuck off," said Dustin. "I swear you're pushing it, Clyde."

"Who's going to take care of Bexley while you work a job?" asked Clyde. "Faith? Hope you don't think I'm a fucking babysitter."

"My boy goes where I go. I can take him to work with me. I know my rights," said Dustin. "What do you think?" he asked Marcus.

"I don't know," said Marcus.

"What if I come by tomorrow?" asked Dustin.

"Talk to him. Why not?" said Marcus.

"See, Clyde? Fucking asshole," said Dustin. Bexley dropped his pacifier, began a high, fluid-filled wail. They finished the beers.

———

Marcus had returned to his trailer and turned up the lantern when the big woman finally came. He saw her appear out of the darkness at the edge of the woods, flickering through the last line of ash trees. She blended momentarily with a sycamore. She separated from it, emerged into the meadow. The big woman had his dead goat yoked around her shoulders and it bled down her front. She wore baggy white polar-fleece pants tucked into the tops of her boots. The pants were covered in burrs, mud, and goat hair. She wore a dun man's coat and a hat with flaps that came down over her ears. She was one of the biggest women Marcus had ever seen. She carried the goat up to his trailer. Marcus spit on his hands, rubbed his face to redden his cheeks, smoothed his hair, opened the door.

"Found this goat in your woods," she said. "It was dead, torn up by the coyotes." She dropped it on his cinderblock steps. Marcus could not think what to say.

"Is it your goat?" she asked. He nodded.

"Please. Stay," he said.

"Here?" she asked. She smelled like vinegar. Up close he could see deep craters on her face, below her left eye.

"Here," he said.

"I can't stay. I'm just resting," she said. "This is my shortcut. I'm going to look at my boy across the road. I heard the coyotes, and I wanted to see what they were after. You know, my name is carved into a tree back there," she said. "Have you seen that?"

"Not yet," said Marcus.

"You been back in your woods at all?" she asked.

"Not yet," said Marcus. "You could show me, maybe?"

The big woman looked at him, screwed up her mouth. "Are you creepy?" she asked.

"No," said Marcus. "I'm just new around here."

"I'll decide for myself," she said. "Maybe later." She looked both ways and strode across the road.

Dustin stepped into the road and waved Marcus down after work. Marcus slowed his truck and rolled the window down. Dustin leaned in on his elbows.

"You want an apple?" Dustin asked, pulling one from the pocket of his sweatshirt.

"That's all right," said Marcus.

"It's a Gold Rush," said Dustin. He bit into it.

"Okay, thanks," said Marcus. He took a bite and handed it back.

"I stopped by Gordo's," said Dustin.

"I didn't see you," said Marcus.

"Well I saw you," said Dustin. "That guy ever put anything away?"

"I don't know," said Marcus. "Did you talk to him about work?"

"Nah, man, that asshole wants me to yell out everything I do as I'm doing it." He stared searchingly at Marcus. "That's right, I heard you doing it, you sorry sap. I've got a shred of dignity left. I may be poor but fuck it, Gordo can shove it up his ass for all I care." Dustin rapped on the roof, took another bite of the apple. "Faith told me she found your goat," he said, chewing and watching Marcus.

"The coyotes found it first," said Marcus, looking at the steering wheel.

"Things are good with me and her now," said Dustin. "Never better."

"Glad to hear it," said Marcus. Dustin stepped back from the truck and put the apple to his mouth. Marcus pulled away, watching him in the rearview mirror. Dustin didn't move until he had eaten the apple down to its core. He stood for a moment, hands at his side, then swiveled, wound up, and pitched the apple core hard against a red oak, so that it flung sparks of white flesh out into the cold.

—

When Marcus saw Faith again, it had been raining all night and all morning, and she was down in the creek trying to get a log out of the culvert. Marcus walked down his driveway, and stopped on the low bridge above her. She looked up at him, rested one end of the log on her shoulder, put her raw red hands on her knees, and breathed. Marcus could see the goat's blood still crusted on her neck and on her dun-colored coat.

"Creepy guy," she said, "culvert's jammed up."

"Do you need help?" he asked.

"Yeah I need help," she said. She laughed. "Dustin won't provide. He wraps Bexley up in T-shirts, won't change his diaper but twice a day 'cause we're running low, don't have money for more. Assistance cut me right off, said I wasn't telling the truth about where I live. It's fucked. It's totally fucked. Wish I could keep Bexley with me but Dustin's dad's the one with the money. I'm just moving from place to place. Odd jobs. You want to see my list, here's my list," she said. With one hand, she dug in her pocket, then reached up to Marcus with a scrap of paper, the log end cradled massively next to her left ear. On the list was diapers, wipes, blankets, towels, onesies, snowsuit, bottles, formula, rent, phone bill.

"Actually what I meant is that I'm worried about you moving that log on your own," said Marcus.

"Get down here then," said Faith.

He came clumsily down the bank. He knelt, reached forward into the creek, and rolled the butt end of the log onto the bank without lifting it. Faith held her end steady.

"Are we going to talk about this?" he asked her.

"Just get it up on the bridge," she said. "Now would be good. This thing's fucking heavy."

"On the count of three?" he asked.

"Just fucking do it," she said. She lowered her end of the soaked log so that it rested against her chest. She clutched it with both arms and began to stagger forward one step at a time, her boots filling with water. Marcus followed her down into the creek, lifting his end of the log, fighting to find any kind of hold on the slimy bark.

"Get on the same side as me, goddammit," Faith gasped. Marcus could not see how to do this, but somehow ducked low and moved underneath the log. He made it to the other side and wrapped both arms around it. "Maybe we should take a rest," he said.

"Fuck you walk forward," said Faith through gritted teeth. They did so and made it to the bridge.

"Push it up," ordered Faith.

"On three," said Marcus.

"I can't hold it anymore, asshole," said Faith, and gave the log a mighty shove up over her head, getting her end onto the bridge. Marcus scrambled to follow her lead but the great weight of the log came down on him, he could no longer hold on, he stumbled out of the way, and his end swung out over the creek. Bodily, Faith shoved against him and got behind the log again, and together they shifted the thing back so that it rolled full length onto the bridge and lay still and dripping. They climbed out and sat on it.

"I'm soaking wet," said Marcus. "Are you okay?"

"You're an idiot," said Faith.

"Are you still married to Dustin?" Marcus asked.

"We have an understanding," said Faith. "He can't tell me what to do. I'm the boss."

Marcus wanted to show her all that he had collected. With a great eager swelling of his heart, he wondered what she would think of the cafeteria table. He liked it because it folded in the middle so that it would store neatly in the house he would build. If ever there was a big family Thanksgiving, they could bring out the long table and unfold it with no hassle. First he would have to affix new hinges because the current ones were rusted through. The sun came out from behind the clouds and the sky was white. The turkey vultures plummeted from vast heights, then flocked back up on banks of wind.

"Do you have my list?" asked Faith. Marcus pressed the piece of paper in his damp breast pocket.

———

Gordo began the day by talking about the pencils that kept slipping from behind his ears. "I told those morons at the hardware store, I have connections," he said.

"They didn't know who you were?" asked Marcus, marking a two-by-eight. He could feel Gordo's eyes on him, suspicious. "People around here, they don't know the people I know," said Gordo. "They look at me and think I'm just some asshole. Everyone around here is such a nobody they think I'm a nobody. But they don't get it that if I made one phone call, I could get them shut down for this pencil shit. I could talk to the top guy and heads would roll. Just one phone call."

"Did you tell them about your wife's FBI clearance?" said Marcus.

Gordo stopped.

"You want to be a wiseass today? Is that it?" said Gordo. "What is that you're doing? Did you forget what I told you?" Marcus called out circular saw. He made the cut. Then Marcus looked at his tools strewn about the first floor of Gordo's mansion. He looked at his chapped hands. He thought about Faith's list. "What are you pausing for? It's my money you're wasting," said Gordo, and started up the table saw. Marcus tilted his head back. He thought about how big Faith was. He thought about her baggy fleece pants. He thought about the goat's blood. Marcus called out piss. At first Gordo didn't hear him. So Marcus called piss louder. "You've got to be loud if you want to keep this goddamm job," said Gordo. So Marcus called out piss as if his wife and child were stuck under a bus and the only way to save them was to call out piss louder than anyone else had ever called out piss. And he did it. He saved them.

Inside Gordo's sweltering dark house, Marcus could hear the screaming son, the ticking of the swing on the upper floor. He paused, let his eyes adjust. Carefully, he took stock of the cases of diapers stacked in the living room next to boxes of powdered formula. In the bathroom, there were rubber ducks in descending sizes, a pair of carmine-red rubber pants, baby nail clippers on the windowsill. There were bouncy chairs, board books, Pat the Bunny and The Very Hungry Caterpillar. On a shelf below the jigsaw puzzle, there were two breast pumps, one manual, one electric. There was a machine that mimicked the rhythm of a mother's heartbeat.

When Gordo unplugged the shop light that night, Marcus asked him, "Mind if I leave my tools inside your house? It's supposed to be below freezing. At least the batteries."

"Whatever," said Gordo, so Marcus took his empty duffle bag inside.

—

On his land, Marcus cut a piece of the large drab net and used it to patch the hole in the trampoline. He got the trampoline up on its legs and inspected the springs. They were rusty but they held when he applied his weight. He swept the trampoline and assembled the safety net around its perimeter. He pulled his folding chair out of his trailer and sat in front of the trampoline, looking at it. He drank a beer, thought it through. He got up and brought his duffle bag from the truck, set it beside the trampoline. He unzipped it, folded open the top, sat back down in his chair, and opened another beer. He looked at the trampoline. He looked at the case of diapers peeking out the top of the duffle bag, nestled beside the carton of baby wipes, a medium-sized rubber duck, a box of formula. The sun began to set. He heard the thieves rev their engines. He smelled the rich rubber smoldering in their campfire. He stayed where he was.

———

When Marcus came back to work, Gordo was pacing back and forth, chewing his lip and shaking his head. He held his roaring hatless boy, whose arms and legs stuck straight out, his small face a mask of discomfort. The boy hit his dad and screamed. Gordo grabbed the boy's hands and forced them to his sides.

"Someone stole my shit," shouted Gordo over his son's cries. Marcus couldn't help it, his stomach lurched. Saliva filled his mouth.

"Two pieces of plywood gone and my transit level. A box of Liquid Nails. Five bags of concrete. What the fuck?"

Marcus exhaled.

"Well?" said Gordo. "Don't you have anything to say?"

"I went to a neighborhood-watch meeting," said Marcus.

"I can't lay the subfloor today. This fucking meth town." The small boy screamed. His face turned purple, but around his eyes his skin was pale.

"What are we going to do today, then?" yelled Marcus.

"We?" said Gordo.

"If we can't lay the subfloor?" asked Marcus.

"There's no 'we,'" said Gordo. "I don't need your kind around here."

"My kind?" asked Marcus.

"Telling all your scumfuck friends to come and load up whatever shit they can carry. My wife says I should press charges," said Gordo.

"Fuck you," said Marcus beneath the son's squall.

"What?" asked Gordo, covering his son's mouth with one hand.

"I quit," called out Marcus. He turned to go.

"Are you stupid?" asked Gordo. "I just fired you," but the boy's screams drowned him out.

———

Marcus waited in his trailer. He stoked up the fire. He poured lamp oil into his lantern. He cut up an apple and some cheese. He watched the apple turn brown. He watched the cheese dry out. The sun went down.

Marcus could hear the thieves shooting beer cans over at their campfire, but he kept the blinds drawn. He heard their joyful hollers, the engines revving on their dirt bikes, the bikes racing up and down the road. Marcus didn't look. His duffle bag sat in the corner, still full. Marcus tucked in his shirt. There was a knock at his door.

Faith stood outside, holding Bexley in his car seat. Bexley was asleep, snoring as loud as a grown man.

"You came," said Marcus.

"Invite me in quick," said Faith. Marcus stood aside and she moved past him into his tiny living space. She set the car seat on the fold-out table. She tossed apples and cheese into her mouth.

"You got a curtain?" she asked through a mouthful, then saw the sofa cushions. "These will do," she said, and built a small pillow fort around the car seat, obscuring Bexley from view. "Let's be discreet," she said.

"I got you some things from your list," said Marcus.

"We can talk about that later," said Faith. "That's not why I'm here. Well, not the full reason. It's more about how we moved the log together."

As she stepped toward him, they heard the dirt bikes roar up and idle at the end of the driveway.

"Don't worry," said Faith. "We like a fight. My money's on you."

"I don't like a fight," said Marcus.

"Just stay quiet," said Faith. They stood still, while Bexley snored and the dirt bikes swarmed around them, on either side of his trailer, churning up the mud. The engines sputtered down and many men dismounted, whispering, stifling laughter. Boots crunched past the trailer window. Faith reached for Marcus. She held him. He let himself be held. They waited. Nothing. They heard the men move past the trailer, then keep moving. Their sounds faded off into the meadow. Many lady beetles landed on the oil lamp. No one came to the door.

"Well," said Faith, stepping back.

"They're on my land," said Marcus. "What are they doing?"

"I guess we got a little time after all," said Faith.

"The only thing is, I'm worried Dustin will kill me," said Marcus.

"I do what I want and Dustin knows that," said Faith. She put her hand down the front of Marcus's pants. "Look," she said. "We're already doing it. This is doing it, it's doing something." Marcus got hard right away but wanted to be polite about it. He wanted things done the right way. He said, "I'm afraid of the dark."

"I don't believe it," Faith said.

"That's because I pretend not to be."

"What's the difference between pretending not to be afraid of the dark and not being afraid of the dark?" she asked.

Marcus put his arms around her. He said, "Have you heard that song I would do anything for love, or what about the musical Oliver. Have you seen that? Do you like musicals? Would you climb a hill, pick a daffodil, because that's how I feel about you, like I would do anything," Marcus said. "I guess there are a lot of songs like that probably, isn't that true? It's a feeling people get, even when they don't know each other very well."

"Yes," she said. "That's the point."

Marcus was afraid and happy. He believed her when she said she was the boss. She went to her knees before him and undid his belt. "Thank you," he said. "Thank you so much."

—

The confrontation Dustin owed Marcus, the interference of the law, the foster care system, the eventual loss of the land—look for it in the public record. The next day would come, and then the next. They would come later. Now, here inside the warm trailer, Bexley snored, and Marcus and Faith murmured. Outside, a great cacophonous groaning rose up, a mechanical wheezing, as if the bellows of the world had opened in Marcus's acreage. In the meadow, the thieves jumped on the trampoline. They were in their stocking feet. Though they meant to be menacing, it was too dark to make out much besides their vigor, their startled laughter, their boots lined up neatly in the bear grass. They wore headlamps, and the lights tossed the shadows around as they leapt up and down. Their faces loomed crazily in and out of sight, showing outsized noses and deep eye sockets. The trampoline itself was a sinking sea of black ink, rising back again and again, lifting them up on its swells so that they sprang into the air.

Madeline ffitch was a founding member of the punk theater company The Missoula Oblongata. She lives and writes in Appalachian Ohio where she homesteads and raises ducks, goats, and her small son, Nector.

ACKNOWLEDGMENTS

"Planet X" was the inspiration for the 2007 Missoula
Oblongata play "The Wonders of the World: Recite," written
by Donna Sellinger and Madeline ffitch, the script of which
was published by Chuckwagon Press in 2007, and toured
nationally and to Canada from 2006 to 2008.
"The Fisher Cat" first appeared in *The Chicago Review*
"What Wants to be Shot" first appeared in *Sententia*
"The Private Fight" first appeared in *The Collagist*
"The Big Woman" first appeared in *Tin House*

Thanks to Chris Bachelder, Noy Holland, Dara Wier, and
Stanley Crawford for reading and believing in and challenging
these stories, and thanks to Cusi Ballew for asking the right
questions always and for telling stories faster than I can write
them.

CPSIA information can be obtained
at www.ICGtesting.com
Printed in the USA
FSHW011210160919

9 780990 602002